The Big Fiddle

An Inspector Angel Mystery

The Big Fiddle

An Inspector Angel Mystery

ROGER SILVERWOOD

ROBERT HALE · LONDON

ISBN 978-0-7198-1033-6

Robert Hale Limited
Clerkenwell House
Clerkenwell Green
London EC1R 0HT

www.halebooks.com

2 4 6 8 10 9 7 5 3 1

B000 000 010 2085

Typeset in 11/16pt Sabon
Printed in the UK by the Berforts Group

ONE

'You wanted to see me, Doc?' Patrick Downey said from the door, trying not to look worried.

The doctor in the white coat looked over his desk and smiled broadly at him. 'Yes. Come in, Patrick. Come in. I have some excellent news for you. Sit down.'

Downey, in pyjamas and dressing gown, sat down in the chair on the other side of the desk.

Dr Macwhinney, still smiling, said, 'I kept telling you that your petitions would not go unheeded.'

Downey blinked and licked his lips.

'This morning I received a report from the visiting board which examined you last week,' Macwhinney said. 'Essentially it says that they saw no trace at all of your personality disorder. Now, that's tremendous news, isn't it? In addition, I note from the house doctor that the dreams have now stopped, also that you are not dependent on any anti-depressive, tranquillizing or other medication. In fact, to show our faith in you, Dr Howitzer, Dr Zimmerman and I have already made the statutory declaration that you are entitled to trial leave according to the Mental Health Act 1983.'

Patrick Downey's mouth dropped open. It was something he

had been waiting to hear for fourteen years. His eyes became moist. He felt in his pocket for a handkerchief, but he couldn't find it. He wiped his eyes with the sleeve of his dressing gown, and then looked down at the floor. 'How soon can I leave then, Doc? Does that mean I can leave today?'

Dr Macwhinney smiled. 'Not quite as quickly as that, Patrick, but quite soon. We have to set up arrangements for you to be able to check in each day—'

Downey's nose turned upward and the corners of his mouth downward. 'You mean so that I don't run off?' he said.

'Not at all,' Macwhinney said. 'It is to see that you are feeling happy and confident, that's all. If you run off, Patrick, it means that the entire panel of doctors have made a gross mistake, and it will show the world that the psychiatric staff at this hospital are completely incompetent. And the press would love to hear *that*, wouldn't they? No, Patrick, the terms of the "trial leave" require you to check with an appropriately accredited doctor, whom we will make familiar with your case. Should he not be able to advise you, he will be able to contact Dr Howitzer or Dr Zimmerman or me 24/7 for the first four weeks of your leave. It's in *your* interests, Patrick. All right?'

Downey accepted what Macwhinney had said. 'Yes,' he said.

Macwhinney beamed and said, 'I know you have been here for twelve years, which is a big chunk out of your life, but you must look on your stay in this hospital as necessary to get well again. I know there are many restrictions here, but they are for everybody's good including your own.'

'Oh, I do. I do. I know how I was. How introverted I was … sullen and depressed. Now I feel a thousand per cent better. And I want to thank you and Dr Howitzer and the entire team for your kindness and professional skill in seeing me through that time and for healing me.'

'It is a delight for us, Patrick, to have a success with you, even though it has taken twelve years. There are 259 other patients in this hospital who still suffer from some sort of paranoid schizophrenia with complications and are living proof, sadly, of our limitations. But ... be that as it may ... now, *you* have to decide on whether you want to go back to your roots in South Yorkshire or start entirely afresh in a different part of the UK. Also, we shall need to create a new identity for you....'

Bromersley High Street, South Yorkshire, UK. 14.00 hours. Saturday, 4 May 2013.

Charles Morris liked women and women liked him: it was a convenient arrangement. He was the sort of man who had women eating out of his hand. When he entered a room, females from eight to eighty turned to look. Most of them continued looking, particularly if he reciprocated by the raising of an eyebrow followed by a shiny white grin.

He looked good, really good, particularly to sexy young women.

Of course, he looked after himself ... always had done. He didn't smoke and drank only rarely. He worked out most days, swam, and then topped up his tan under a lamp.

His suits came from Savile Row and his car was a new Jaguar XJL.

His manners were impeccable, his anticipation matchless. If madam accidentally knocked a cup off the table, it was Charles who would catch it and avoid the breakage. If a door needed opening, Charles had his hand on the handle ready. If she needed more cream in her coffee, Charles would already be passing the jug.

He had moved to Bromersley recently and lived in a well-appointed apartment in an old vicarage that had been converted into six luxury units. It was located in a large garden on the outskirts of Bromersley at the foot of the Pennines.

That Saturday afternoon, he had an arrangement to meet up with the present light of his life, Moira Elsworth. She was quite the prettiest girl in town and he was mad about her. She was always on his mind. He could think of nothing else for long. She had those long, curvy legs that men like to see and caress.

He had parked the car and was standing on the busy pavement under the clock outside Jeeves, the jewellers. He had arranged to meet her there at noon. They had planned to have lunch together, but she was already five minutes late. He knew that Moira had intended visiting her mother and was then coming on by bus from there.

Moira had been living with her mother, Christine Elsworth. Christine had turned a few heads in her time, but at fifty-six, the years were taking their toll. She had a small flower kiosk on the fringe of the town. She had married Grant Elsworth in her thirties. Grant had been a clerk in the council tax office in Bromersley Town Hall. He had worked his way up to chief clerk, but tragically had died eight years ago, leaving Christine a widow at the early age of forty-eight. They had had one daughter, Moira, now twenty, who had inherited the most attractive physical features of her mother and her late father.

Christine Elsworth's time was fully taken up looking after her 92-year-old invalid father and the little flower kiosk. Moira had lived with her in an old, squashed, back-to-back terraced house in the middle of a thousand other squashed, back-to-back houses, with windows that looked out on to grimy red brick walls. There wasn't a tree, bush, blade of grass or dandelion in sight. Moira had detested the place.

People pushed past Charles, with their shopping bags or parcels, sometimes carelessly hitting him on the knee or back with their purchases. He looked at his watch. It said twelve minutes past twelve. He stamped his feet on the flagstones and looked round in all directions for Moira but she was nowhere to be seen. He was certain the arranged meeting time was noon. He couldn't think of any reason why she wasn't there. He hoped she hadn't been taken ill or anything like that. It would drive him mad if anything happened to her. You heard such strange things these days. It could just happen to Moira. Not long since on a bus in Leeds, some 20-year-old nutcase with a knife murdered a 17-year-old girl as she was travelling to college. She had died in seconds. Ghastly state of affairs. He prayed that such a thing could not have happened to Moira.

He peered through the crowd and then there was a tall woman with silky blonde hair and his pulse raced. She was advancing towards him. But it wasn't Moira. He frowned, checked his watch again and shook his head. She was sixteen minutes late.

Suddenly, from behind, he felt a touch on his arm and a breathy voice said, 'Hello, darling.'

It was Moira. The relief!

He turned, arms outstretched. They glanced at each other, sighed and wrapped themselves together in a kiss that they held for several seconds.

Shoppers and passers-by barely gave them a glance as they bustled past along the busy pavement.

Eventually he pulled away from her. 'Are you all right? I was getting so worried.'

She laughed and her eyes twinkled. 'Oh, yes. Do you know what, Charles? I met a girl in my mum's shop. We went to junior school together.'

He looked at her. She didn't seem to care that he had been so worried.

I haven't seen her since we were twelve,' she said, 'and she recognized me straightaway. She recalled all sorts of things that happened to us that I had almost forgotten. Isn't that fantastic?'

Charles wasn't at all interested.

'Are we having lunch together or not?' he asked.

She noticed the coolness. 'Er ... yes, if that's all right, Charles. That is what we ... er, planned.'

'Yes, but I wondered if you wanted to do anything different. I mean, if you wanted us to find that schoolfriend and have her join us for lunch ... if she's that interesting.'

She looked at him uncertainly and licked her bottom lip with the tip of her tongue. After a second, she said, 'No. It's not that she was particularly interesting, but I hadn't seen her for eight years and ... it's not at all important, Charles darling, I was just telling you what happened because ... erm, well, I thought you might be interested. But that's all right. Let's go for lunch.'

'You don't seem a bit concerned that I've been standing here for sixteen minutes waiting, worrying and wasting time.'

'Oh, darling, I'm sorry. I hadn't realized. Yes, of course, you have.'

'Thank you. It's a bit much that I have to point out that you're very late ... because of you meeting up with an old schoolfriend and chatting away. I was thinking that something dreadful had happened to you.'

Moira pursed her lips. 'She was a very good friend to me. We were together from nursery school.'

'So you think it's all right to stand me up like a fool, worrying about whether you'd be run down by a bus, or something worse?'

'I didn't stand you up. I'm here now. Are we going to have a meal together or not?'

'You're really not a bit sorry. You could have phoned me and made an alternative arrangement, or made a date to see her another time.'

'I didn't plan this. It happened just as I was coming out of the shop.'

'Come on,' Charles said, grabbing her arm. He wanted to say a lot more, but he could see that Moira was not going to climb down any further and he didn't want to lose her. Although she was living with him, she could easily move back in with her mother, and he wasn't willing to be even one night away from her.

They picked their way through the shoppers along the pavement.

She looked up at him and sighed. She must not take the argument to its end as she didn't want to win the argument and lose the man. He could easily pick up another woman and she shouldn't rely on her slick replies to get her out of trouble.

'Where do you want to go?' he asked.

'I'll leave it to you.'

'Depends whether you're hungry or not.'

She breathed in, thought a moment and said, 'Do you know, darling, I'm not that hungry.'

He sighed. That was an answer he hadn't expected. Since he had known her she had always said that she was starving.

They were passing a sandwich bar.

He pointed to it. 'A turkey salad wrap?'

She nodded and smiled.

They came away from the bar with two turkey salad wraps in a bag. Charles smiled and said, 'My car's in the car park round the corner. Let's pick it up.'

She relaxed; the storm had abated.

They got in the Jaguar. When the doors were closed, he leaned over and kissed her gently on the lips, hoping that he had not come on too strong about her being late. She seemed to be settled now.

'Shall we go home, have some coffee with these wraps … and relax?'

She thought *relax* was a euphemism for sex. She was uncertain but she said, 'That would be lovely.'

He smiled, put the car in gear and drove out of the car park. It was slow work getting out of the town centre, but, once away, he made good time on the ring road.

'Tonight, Moira, we can go out to the Feathers,' he said, as he changed up to top gear. 'I'll book a table for 7.30. That'll give us plenty of time together. What do you say?'

'I don't know,' she repeated. She wanted to climb down without losing face. And she desperately wanted his caresses, his embraces, and especially his reassurance, but she also wanted to teach him that she wasn't a cheap and easy lay.

He thought she was thawing. He ran a hand experimentally along her thigh. At first she stiffened, then relaxed and sighed. Indescribable warmth surged upwards into her bosom.

He breathed out. The muscles of his chest and stomach also relaxed and he smiled. He was glad the battle was over and that he had won. At least, he thought he had won.

22 Jubilee Park Road, Bromersley, South Yorkshire, UK. 15.00 hours. Saturday, 4 May 2013.

'Thousands and thousands,' the 92-year-old man muttered from his wheelchair. His thin, white fingers shook, and his dull eyes shone as his mind drifted in and out of the mists of memory.

'Now, Mr Piddington, let's settle you down,' Nancy Quinn, his pretty young part-time carer, said as she pushed him out of the kitchen, down the hall and through the door into his sitting room. She manoeuvred the wheelchair into a position by a table and opposite the television.

'Thousands and thousands,' he continued muttering.

Nancy Quinn pulled on the handbrake.

'You keep saying that,' she said, 'but you don't say *where* it is now.'

'Thousands and thousands,' Piddington continued.

'But where is it *now*?'

'Where? That's it. That's what they never found out. But *I know*. There're thousands and thousands. Do you know, I could go and live in Majorca.'

'You could probably *buy* Majorca, Mr Piddington,' she said as she wiped down the table top. 'All that sunshine would do you the world of good.' An idea crossed her mind. She sniggered. 'I could come with you. That would be nice, wouldn't it? Be your fancy piece?' she said and lifted her blue overall up three inches suggestively. 'You know, I could be really nice to you.'

Far away in his own reminiscences, his white face was expressionless as his watery eyes looked into hers. 'Thousands and thousands.'

Her young face straightened. She went close up to him and looked into his eyes. '*Where* is it, Mr Piddington? *Where* is it?'

'Thousands and thousands.'

She pulled an angry face. 'Aw!' She shook her head impatiently. Then she said, 'Look, Mr Piddington, it's time I was off. Have you taken your pills?'

'What? Yes,' he said. Then he frowned. 'Have I?'

'All of them?'

He looked at her blankly.

'Aw!' she said again. She reached out to a tray on the table which had twenty or thirty boxes and bottles of pills. She glanced at some of the labels, then looked inside the container at some of the contents, then fastened them up and said, 'Yes. I think you must have. Right, I'm going.'

He stared at her, his mouth opened and a stream of saliva dropped from his top set down his chin.

She impatiently snatched a tissue from the box on the table at his side and brusquely wiped his chin and mouth.

He didn't seem to notice what she was doing. His face looked vacant again as he muttered, 'Thousands and thousands.'

'I know. I know! *I know!!*' she screamed. 'You silly old duffer. You're doing my head in. I gotta go. I gotta go.'

Piddington hardly noticed her outburst.

She rushed out of the room, into the hall and up the stairs.

The old man watched her go out and then frowned. He wearily glanced round the room, looked across the table, then patted his dressing gown pockets. He found the remote control for the television, vaguely pressed a button and a picture of horses jumping over fences came up on the screen. He watched them intently. He liked horse racing.

A minute later, there was the sound of a distant toilet being flushed. Nancy Quinn came down the stairs and into the sitting room. She was wearing a raincoat over her uniform and had a handbag hanging from her shoulder.

'Now, Mr Piddington,' she said, 'I'm off. Christine will be here soon. See you tomorrow.'

He didn't answer. He was watching a replay of the end of last month's Grand National.

The front door slammed.

The picture on the television soon changed to a newsreader. He tried to interest himself in it, but he couldn't. He closed his eyes to rest them and fell asleep.

The next thing he remembered was a female voice in the distance: 'Dad. Dad! I've got some tea for you. Don't you want it? Dad. Come on.'

He reached consciousness and his hands and his chest began shaking.

He opened his eyes.

His daughter, Christine Elsworth, was standing at the side of the wheelchair with a beaker in her hand. 'It's all right. It's me, Dad. Do you want this tea?'

He peered up at her, then reached out for the beaker. The shaking stopped.

'There you are,' she said.

Piddington sipped the tea. Christine Elsworth had made it sweet, just how he liked it.

'You must have had a heavy sleep,' she said. 'I've been here about ten minutes. I've brought your tea. It's in the oven keeping hot, till you're ready.' She glanced at the tray of pills on the table. 'Hmm. Where are those pills you have to take before meals? Ah, here they are.' She pressed one out of the plastic packaging and put it into his hand.

He glanced at it and put it in his mouth.

She watched him swallow it and follow it up with another sip of tea.

'Moira sends her love. She's got a new boyfriend. Only known him a week. Moved in with him. He seems a bit old for her. He seems to be well off, though. And I can't do anything with her. She's over eighteen. She's got the law on her side, so she says. Are you listening to me, Dad?'

He nodded and took another sip.

'I think you're a bit better this afternoon, aren't you?' she said.

She often said that to try to keep him cheerful.

'Do you *feel* better?' she said, trying to get him to speak.

He gave her a brief smile, nodded, then straightened his face, looked down at his white, skinny hands and shook his head.

Christine was disappointed. 'Why don't you speak, Dad. I know you *can* still speak if you want to.'

'Mmmm,' he began.

She smiled at him and brushed her hand through his thin, white hair. 'Go on,' she said. 'Now what is it you want to say?'

He took a deep breath and said, 'There're thousands and thousands of pounds.'

Christine Elsworth shook her head. The corners of her mouth turned downward. 'Not *that* again,' she said.

Then again, louder and with enthusiasm Piddington said, 'Thousands and thousands. *Thousands and thousands.*'

TWO

30 Park Street, Forest Hill Estate, Bromersley. 14.00 hours. Sunday, 5 May 2013.

Inspector Michael Angel was at home in his sitting room in jogging trousers and sports shirt, catching up with his reading of the local weekly paper, the *Bromersley Chronicle*.

He had just cleared two helpings of roast beef, Yorkshire pudding, roast potatoes and sprouts followed by a generous helping of fresh fruit salad, and was thoroughly enjoying the peace of the day while his wife, Mary, was in the kitchen banging pans about and slamming cupboard doors.

Eventually she appeared carrying two beakers of coffee. She put them down on coasters on the library table between them.

'Thank you, sweetheart,' he said, without looking up. Then he added, 'Here, Mary, listen to this.'

He read: '"The International Jewellery Fair is being held in Leeds on May 14th to the 19th. Lord and Lady Tulliver from Tunistone will be there to open the fair on Wednesday at 10 a.m. Lady Tulliver will be wearing the Mermaid Diamond."'

He looked up at her. 'What do you think of that?'

Mary said, 'I don't think her ladyship will be *selling* it, darling.'

'Pity,' Angel said. 'I was trying to think of something nice for you for our anniversary.'

She smiled.

'No,' he went on, 'but you would have thought that the people employed as security to the fair would have advised us about it,' he said. 'I've not heard a word about an *international* jewellery fair. Every crook in the area will be thinking how he can get hold of Tulliver's diamond or some other enticing bits of booty.'

'There's time yet,' Mary said. 'And it isn't in Bromersley, it's in Leeds, that's twenty miles away.'

'That's twelve minutes in a Lamborghini.'

'Anyway, I wonder why that diamond is called the "Mermaid" Diamond?'

'I dunno. It says more on page ten. Just a second.' He lifted the paper up and quickly turned over some pages. 'Mmm. It's here. Shall I read it to you? … It says,

"One of the most dazzling exhibits in the Schumacher Museum in South Africa was a 39-carat diamond. It became known as the Mermaid Diamond, because in 1760 a 10-year-old girl found it while playing in a stream. A local sheep farmer heard of this and claimed the stone for himself. In 1768 it was used as barter to secure the release of a lover of Marie Antoinette from the guillotine. Thereafter, the stone changed hands many times and in 1939 it was loaned to the Schumacher Museum by the railway millionaire Henri Van Musdomen who had had it made into a pendant and had presented it to the Princess Farina of Persia on the day of their marriage.

"Over the years, several attempts to steal the many treasures of the Schumacher were foiled by the security systems put in place by the directors of the museum. The cleaners, tellers and workmen at the museum were even subjected to a strip-search and X-ray before leaving at the end of their shifts.

"However, on 2 May 1986, a 46-year-old employee, Moses

Black, a cleaner, who was polishing the showcase where the Mermaid Diamond and other precious jewels were exhibited, forced open the cabinet, took the stone and fastened it to the leg of a homing pigeon he had smuggled into the museum in a container attached to his leg. He then released the bird through an aperture he made by springing back a segment of a ventilation fan on a window in a staff lavatory, and the diamond was on its way to the tiny pigeon loft he had at his primitive corrugated-iron house two miles away.

"Since that time, the diamond has not been seen nor heard of until April 2009 when it was offered for sale in a Swiss auction house, and it was bought for an undisclosed sum by Lord Tulliver of Marlborough House, Tunistone."'

Angel lowered the paper and looked across at Mary. With eyebrows raised, he said, 'Must be worth millions!'

Mary wrinkled her nose. 'You know, Michael, on reflection I won't have that for our anniversary. I wouldn't know where to keep it. And I wouldn't sleep at night knowing that there were people out there wanting to break in and steal it.'

'Lady Tulliver doesn't keep it in a tin box under the bed, sweetheart, nor even in a combination wall safe behind a picture of a hunting scene, drinking the stirrup cup or whatever. Those days are over. Her ladyship will wear it for show at special occasions, when there will be a security man, or a team, watching over her. The rest of the time it will be in a bank vault, in a safe-deposit box. Everybody makes their own arrangements, which of course they keep quiet about.'

'Yes. I see that. It's too much of a chore and a worry for me.'

'The insurance company do all the worrying, darling.'

'For a great deal of money, I expect.'

'Well, yes. But that is what they are for. It's their business.'

'And jolly good luck to them,' she said, and reached out for a magazine she had been reading earlier.

Angel returned to the paper.

They read quietly for a minute or so, then Mary said, 'In a standard pack of playing cards, which king is the only king without a moustache?'

Angel said, 'That's an old one: it's the King of Hearts.'

'Is it? Well, thank you, darling.'

He frowned, looked up and said, 'What *are* you doing?'

'It's a competition.'

'A competition? You're wasting your time. You'll never win anything. They're all devised to sell or advertise something – not give anything worth having away.'

'I know. I know. But you sometimes get nice prizes. There's a woman in Rhyl – a Mrs James – who won fifteen hundred pounds last month.'

'You don't want to take any notice of that. They make it up. Do you know Mrs James of Rhyl?'

'Of course not, but somebody will. There's a photograph of her.'

'If there *is* such a person. It could be anybody. That photo could be the boss's grandmother who lived in Sussex and died ten years ago.'

'You do have a fertile imagination.'

'It's not worth the postage … do you realize what a second-class stamp costs these days?'

'How did we get to this? I only asked you a question about kings on playing cards.'

'We've got to watch our costs, Mary,' he said.

'Are you going to cut the lawn, before it rains?' she said. 'The clouds are building up, and there are a lot of dandelions that want rooting out.'

Angel buried his head back in the newspaper.

The Police Station, Bromersley. 08.28 hours. Monday, 6 May 2013.

Angel arrived at his small office, closed the door, threw his hat at the plastic hook glued onto the side of the green metal cabinet. The brown fedora landed on the hook and stayed there. He looked at it almost in disbelief and he smiled briefly. He looked down at the pile of post on his desk and pulled a face: his nose went up and the corners of his mouth turned downward. He sat down in the swivel chair and began to riffle through them when the phone went.

He reached out for it. 'Angel,' he said.

It was Sergeant Clifton in the control coom. 'Good morning, sir. Sorry to bother you so early, but a woman phoned in a triple nine at 08.10 hours to say that she found her father dead at his home.'

Angel rubbed a hand across his mouth. 'How did he die?'

'Don't know, sir. She's the daughter, next of kin. She was very distressed. It wasn't easy talking to her.'

Angel nodded. He could understand that. 'Has a doctor been summoned?'

'Oh yes, sir. He examined him and pronounced him dead.'

'The daughter is still at the house, I take it, and the body is still there?'

'Yes, sir. I sent Bravo Romeo Two, that's Sean Donohue. He's a good lad. You'll want SOCO, Dr Mac and your sergeants, I take it. Do you want me to alert them?'

'Yes please, Bernie. I'll go there straightaway. What's the name and address?'

'Christine Elsworth, 22 Jubilee Park Road.'

As Angel drove the BMW along Park Road looking for number 22, he saw Bravo Romeo Two standing outside a house next to a small black Ford car. He pulled across the road and parked behind the police car.

Number 22 was small, detached and stone fronted. He knocked on the front door, opened it and walked in.

Two faces turned round to look at him, the police patrolman, Sean Donohue, and a woman. Her eyes were red and moist, and she looked weary. He assumed she was Mrs Christine Elsworth.

Behind her on the floor at the bottom of the stairs, he saw the body of a small, old man in pyjamas and dressing gown. His head was resting on a cushion. His eyes were closed and his face and hair were white. Beside him was a wheelchair on its side.

The patrolman who was holding a pen and a notebook saluted. Angel acknowledged the salute, turned to Christine and said, 'I take it this is Mrs Elsworth?'

'Yes, sir. Good morning, sir,' Donohue said. He turned to the woman and said, 'This is Inspector Angel.'

Angel went up to her and said, 'Mrs Elsworth, I am very sorry to hear of your loss.'

She nodded and said, 'I hope you are going to find out who is responsible?'

The muscles of his mouth and chin tightened. 'I'll do my best,' he said, then he said, 'Did *you* find your father's body?'

'Yes,' she said. 'I called in about thirty-five minutes ago, it would be. I last saw Dad alive at about 5.30 yesterday afternoon. Nancy Quinn should have been in and settled him down last night from six to seven. Made sure he was comfortable ... given him a drink ... filled his hot water bottle ... made sure he had taken his pills ... put his phone handy... checked the windows and locked the door ... and so on.'

'And was the door locked this morning?'

'No. And it's not the first time she's forgotten.'

'And was your father exactly where he is now?'

'He was on his side facing away from the wheelchair. I turned him on his back to make him more comfortable and I put the pillow under his head.'

'So you came in at approximately 8.25. You were naturally shocked and distressed. You moved his position slightly to make him more comfortable.... Didn't you think he was dead?'

'I *knew* he was dead. I could tell from the expression on his face ... and the fact that he was cold.'

'So you didn't phone for a doctor?'

'I did. The first thing I did. I phoned for his GP. And then I dialled 999 and asked for the police.'

Angel rubbed his chin. 'So what do you think happened, then?'

Christine Elsworth said, 'It's obvious what happened. Somebody took my father upstairs in the wheelchair, then let it go. He certainly could not have taken the chair up there himself.'

Angel pursed his lips. 'And who might have done that, Mrs Elsworth, and why?'

'Well the only person who had access to my father was the girl who was his part-time carer, Nancy Quinn.'

'And why would she do that?'

'Who knows? Young people are all alike these days. Drunk or drugged up to their eyeballs. Brainless yobs, most of them ... all they know about is sex, money and drugs.'

'Are you saying that Nancy Quinn, your father's carer, was like that?'

She hesitated then said, 'Well, maybe.'

'Why didn't you do something about it?' Angel said.

'I've tried. God knows I've tried. She's the third carer I've had for him since Christmas. They don't stay long. And I pay well above the going rate.'

Angel pursed his lips, then turned to Donohue. 'Where's the doctor?'

'He's been and gone, sir. He left the death certificate. I have it here.'

'Right, Sean,' Angel said. 'Hang on to it for now.' Then he turned back to Christine Elsworth. 'Was this .... is this Nancy Quinn unreliable?' he said.

'No,' she said, after a moment's thought. 'No, I wouldn't say she was *un*reliable.'

'So ... is she due to call on your father today?'

'Oh yes, indeed she is,' she said. 'In fact she should be here at ten o'clock.' She looked at her watch. 'And I'm very late opening my shop. Not that it matters *that* much. But if there's nothing else you need from me, Inspector, I'd better go and open it. Of course, if there *is* anything, I'll stay.'

Angel said, 'Will you call in to the station sometime soon to have your fingerprints taken, Mrs Elsworth? It's so that SOCO can eliminate your prints from the crime scene. And I will want to interview you at length later. You get off, if you will be all right on your own?'

'Oh yes,' she said. 'I will be better working than being here.'

'Is there anybody else who calls regularly or works here who might have called in to see your father since last night?'

'No. I can't think of anybody. The last time I saw him was at about 5.30 ... oh dear.' She began to cry again.

Angel nodded. He patted her on her arm and said, 'Right, Mrs Elsworth, that's all for now. Leave the phone numbers and addresses where I can reach you ... with Patrolman Donohue.'

'I've already got all that, sir,' Donohue said.

'And I will need the address and phone number of the old gentleman's carer, Nancy Quinn,' Angel said.

'I've got that as well, sir.'

Angel nodded with satisfaction at Donohue.

'I'll be back later, Inspector,' she said.

'Yes. I shall need to see you today for a statement.'

She took a longing look at the body of her father, swallowed hard and went out.

Angel glanced at his watch. It was 9.50. He had it in mind that if Nancy Quinn *had* pushed old Mr Piddington down the stairs, as was suggested by Christine Elsworth, she might not come to work at ten o'clock that morning. Then again, if she wanted to brazen it out, perhaps she *would* come. Whatever happened, he wanted to be certain to see her reaction to the news that the old man was dead.

He turned to Donohue. 'Sean, tell me, what did you find when you arrived?'

Donohue turned back a few pages in his notebook and said, 'Well, sir, I got here at 08.43 hours to find Mrs Elsworth on her knees in tears, putting a cushion – that cushion – under her father's head. I immediately put my hand to his neck; there was no pulse, and he was very cold, so I knew he was a goner. I phoned back to our control room and reported what I'd found. Sergeant Clifton said he'd notify the super. Then a few minutes later you arrived.'

'Yes, Sean, I've got all that, but what was the scene like? I mean, the old man didn't have his head on a pillow, did he?'

'No, sir. Mrs Elsworth put it there.'

'What I want to know is – where exactly was he?'

'Pretty much where he is now, sir.'

'And what do you think happened?'

Donohoe looked at Angel and frowned. 'Well, I dunno, sir. I suppose he accidentally took his wheelchair over the edge of the top step and came tumbling down the stairs.'

'Do you think he came down in the wheelchair and fell out at the bottom?'

'I honestly don't know, sir. It seems to me it doesn't matter. I think he came down the stairs at speed and was killed by the fall.'

'It does matter, Sean. It matters a lot. Anyway, thank you for your help.'

There was the sound outside of vehicles arriving.

'Sounds like the cavalry,' Angel said. 'You'd better get off home. I know you've been up all night.'

'I've written out those addresses and phone numbers of Mrs Elsworth and Nancy Quinn, sir,' he said, tearing a page out of his notebook and handing it over to him.

Angel took it, glanced at it, nodded and shoved it into his pocket. 'Thank you, lad,' he said, 'and give that death certificate to Ahmed in the CID office before you go, will you?'

'Right, sir,' Donohue said and he went quickly out of the front door.

Angel looked around the hall to make sure he hadn't over-looked anything, then he crossed to the front door and opened it.

The SOCO van and Dr Mac's car and the mortuary van were parked outside on Jubilee Park Road. DS Donald Taylor, head of SOCO at Bromersley, was coming through the gate. Angel opened the door wide and indicated to him to come into the hall.

Taylor saw the dead man and the mess at the bottom of the stairs.

'Hmm. I see,' Taylor said. 'Not very nice, sir.'

Angel said, 'I'm afraid that the scene has been contaminated by the daughter, Don. She found him. And there's nothing we could have done about it. Also a GP has been over him to examine him to issue a death certificate.'

Taylor nodded thoughtfully. He shook his head. He wasn't pleased, but he smiled. 'Well, sir, we've dealt with worse situations, haven't we?'

'If you take away the pillow under his head, the scene would be about as accurate as we can make it.'

'Right,' he said. 'I'll go out and get togged up.' He turned round and went back out of the front door.

Angel checked his watch. It was 9.57. He was thinking about that young carer, Nancy Quinn. He went up to the door again. Then he saw his old Glaswegian friend Dr Mac coming up the path.

'Good morning, Michael,' he said. 'What a beautiful day for doing a spot of fishing in the Spey?'

'Too early in the year for me, Mac. It would be too cold, I'm afraid.'

'Ye would have to bring a bottle of Glenfinnan in your pocket. That would keep you warm. Now what have you got for me this time?'

'You're a bit premature, Mac. SOCO haven't done their stuff yet. Anyway, come in.'

Angel stood back to allow the doctor through.

Mac saw the dead man and the wheelchair on its side. 'Oh, I see. Hmm. What happened, then? Has he come down the stairs in the wheelchair?'

'He was very old, Mac. He was ninety-two.'

The doctor's grey, bushy eyebrows shot up. 'Really! It's a great age. A very great age. You know, this could be accidental death, Michael.'

'Could be; however, the daughter said that he hadn't the strength to pull the chair upstairs himself, suggesting that some person possibly took the chair up with him in it. Fingerprints on the chair might show who that might have been. Having reached the top, the chair was then accidentally or deliberately pushed off the landing. It sailed down the stairs, and didn't apparently turn over until it hit the bottom. At least, that's what it looks like.'

Mac screwed up his grey, bushy eyebrows and peered up the staircase. 'It's a fair fall, that, Michael. It could finish anybody off if they fell from the top up there.'

Angel nodded. 'Apparently he had no call to go upstairs. I understand that everything the old chap needed was downstairs. This house even has a downstairs loo.'

DS Taylor came bustling in with three others from SOCO. They were all dressed in white sterile overalls, caps and wellingtons. Two of them were carrying large white holdalls.

'Excuse me, gentlemen,' Taylor said.

Angel and Mac moved back towards the front door.

Taylor looked at Angel and said, 'I know it's a bit late, but I'll tape off the area round the bottom of the stairs, the steps themselves and the landing at the top. We'll treat that area as the possible crime scene, sir, if you agree?'

Angel nodded. 'Whatever you think, Don.'

Taylor seemed to like the answer. He smiled and rushed off with a roll of 2"-wide plastic tape that was printed blue on white: CRIME SCENE – DO NOT CROSS. He started wrapping it round furniture and sticking it to wherever he could with Sellotape.

Angel and Mac edged further towards the front door. Angel looked at his watch. 'What time do you make it, Mac?'

'It's ten o'clock on the button.'

'Aye, that's what I make it.'

Angel opened the front door and looked out. 'Mr Piddington's carer is due here at ten,' he said.

Mac said, 'If you'll excuse me, Michael, I might as well get kitted up. I don't think Don will be long round the body.'

'Yes, right, Mac. Talk to you later.'

Mac went out.

Angel held the door open for him. The doctor made his way down the path.

A car slowed down and stopped.

Angel's eyebrows went up. He peered across the tiny front

garden to the gate. A young woman appeared. It was Detective Sergeant Flora Carter, one of two sergeants who were on Angel's team, and quite the most beautiful member of the Bromersley force.

He was pleased to see her, but he urgently wanted to see Nancy Quinn. She should have been there, at 22 Jubilee Park Road, attending the old man. He hoped that she had not done a bunk. It could take years to find her. Access to the world was comparatively easy these days, and many countries had no extradition arrangements with the UK. He felt in his pocket to find the page torn out of Sean Donohue's notebook. He peered at it and checked Nancy Quinn's address. He nodded and went out of the door, closing it after himself. He met Flora Carter at the gate.

'Good morning, sir,' Flora said. 'Came as soon as I could.'

'Hmmm. Where's Crisp? Have you seen him on your travels?'

'No, sir. Not this morning.'

Angel wrinkled his nose. He wasn't pleased. 'Never can find that lad. I don't know what he gets up to.'

Flora nodded.

Angel said, 'I want you to go with me to investigate, and possibly bring in for questioning, the victim's carer, a lass called Nancy Quinn. We'll go in my car.'

THREE

Ernest Potter and Son, Estate Agents, Victoria Road, Bromersley.
10.00 hours. Monday, 6 May 2013.

Adrian Potter was sitting at his desk. He had dealt with the post. It had only been bills and another circular letter from Sun Life. He wasn't a bit interested in life insurance, but they *were* offering a free Parker pen for enquiring. He would think about that. It might just be worth answering the ad to get the free Parker pen. He looked at the computer monitor, and checked the Inbox on his emails. There was nothing there needing a reply. His paperwork was up to date, there had been nothing to file, and there was nothing on the voicemail. He'd had two cups of tea. He leaned back in the swivel chair, put his feet on the edge of the wastepaper bin and yawned. It wasn't long before his eyes glazed over and he began to think about money and then girls. Girls and money.

He was thinking how much of both he could have if he really could sell thousands of houses or, alternatively, rob a small bank. It was possible. It was *quite* possible. If you thought about it long enough anything was possible. He could just see himself all bronzed up on a yacht in the blazing sun in the Mediterranean drinking champagne with half a dozen hipless beauties waiting on him hand and foot, and not another man for miles. The sun's rays would do him the world of good. He was already feeling warmer, important and powerful. Money meant power. And power meant girls. He looked in the mirror and flashed his teeth. He wrinkled his nose and flashed them again. How great it would be to have his teeth covered at the front with bleached white veneers. He was wondering where he could have it done in Bromersley when the phone rang.

His mouth dropped open with shock as he was dragged back to reality. He sucked in a lungful of air, turned up the corners of his mouth to simulate a smile, coughed very lightly to clear his throat, reached out and grabbed the phone. 'Good morning, Ernest Potter and Son, Adrian Potter speaking, can I help you?' he said.

'I am thinking of moving into the area,' the caller said. 'I am looking for a small detached house with a garage near Jubilee Park. It doesn't matter what the superficial condition is, provided that it is reflected in the price. I intend to do it up from top to bottom anyway. My name is Edward Oliver, by the way.'

'Well, let me see, Mr Oliver, we have more than a dozen properties that might fill the bill.'

'Anything on Jubilee Park Road?'

'Mmmm. Nothing actually on Jubilee Park Road. I have one round the corner on Park View. That's a small detached house. And it has a garage. And another further down the road which has room for a garage. I have some very attractive properties in all districts of Bromersley. Why don't you call in sometime, Mr Oliver?'

'I live out of town and I am all over the place, Mr Potter, but if I give you my mobile number, would you be kind enough to give me a ring if anything on Jubilee Park Road comes in during the next week or so?'

'With pleasure. And in the meantime, I'll go through our portfolio myself and let you have brochures of the properties near to the park for your interest, if you would let me have your address.'

'No. I don't need all that, thank you.'

Potter was surprised by the man's response, but he took the mobile number Oliver offered him gladly, made all the noises one would make to a new, prospective customer and ended the phone call.

Angel checked the address of Nancy Quinn given to him by Police Patrolman Donohue and then stuffed the notebook sheet into his pocket. It wasn't far, four or five minutes in the BMW. On the journey, he briefed Flora Carter on the case to date. She asked one or two pointed questions and by the time they reached Sheffield Road, she was fully conversant with the case and with Angel's ideas and opinions.

The address of Nancy Quinn's flat was Commodore House on Commodore Street, which was on the right. It was a large block of flats that had been built – or thrown up – in the 1960s to try to end the great shortage of housing there had been in the town. It was an off-white concrete monster built where slums had been.

Angel pulled up outside the building. Several small children were playing ball games. One older lad was drawing matchstick men on the outside wall with white chalk. He saw Angel and Carter and ran off.

'That little monster should have been in school, I reckon,' Angel said.

It amused Flora Carter, but she kept a straight face. 'Do you want me to chase him, sir?' she said.

Angel looked grim. He shook his head. 'We've bigger fish to fry, lass,' he said.

They found the lift, which had graffiti all over the doors. Angel pressed the button and was amazed to find the mechanism working. When the lift cage arrived and the doors opened, the inside was an eye-dazzling spectacle of bright colours, naked figures, and faces. It was peppered with swear words, some with very creative spelling.

They rattled up to the first floor, then wandered along a corridor with many doors. There were tiny screw holes in the woodwork of the doors where Angel imagined metal or plastic numbers had at one time been fixed; now a daubing of black paint indicated the flat numbers. Eventually they found number 21.

Angel pressed the green button and they heard it noisily ring 'ding-dong.' As they waited, he turned to Flora and said, 'I hope this woman hasn't run off. It would make life so difficult.'

Flora nodded. She knew it would.

He rang the doorbell again, several times in quick succession.

They waited. There was still no response.

A woman came out of a nearby flat. She looked them both up and down, then walked away quickly towards the lift.

When the sound of the lift was out of their hearing, and all was quiet, Flora noticed that Angel was looking down the corridor, his eyes almost motionless. She knew he was listening. She didn't know the reason.

'What's the matter, sir?' she said.

In a whisper he said, 'Keep your eyes and ears open. Let me know if anybody is coming.'

He looked quickly left and then right.

'Why, sir?' she said. 'What are you going to do?'

He looked at her, shook his head and said, 'You don't want to know.'

Then he reached into his pocket, took out a plastic card, inserted it in the gap between the door and the door jamb in line with the lock and gave it a sharp tap with the palm of his hand. At the same moment, he turned the doorknob, applied pressure to the door and the latch was pushed back enough to allow the door to be unlocked. He pushed it open a few inches.

Flora looked at him wide-eyed and said, 'So that's how it's done?'

'Well ... don't tell anybody,' he said.

Angel recovered the plastic card, put it in his pocket, pushed open the door and looked into the little room.

He saw a mess of arms, legs and hair, partly clad, on the floor, in the middle of a pool of blood. Also one of the walls was smeared with blood. His stomach came up to his mouth and he drew in a deep breath.

Flora Carter saw the scene from behind him. A cold shiver ran down her spine. 'Oh my God,' she said.

Angel and Flora Carter had no time to nurture their shock.

'Wait here, Flora,' he said, then he took four steps into the room, peered at the blood-covered face of the young woman, touched her neck, then tiptoed back out of the room and pulled the door to.

In the corridor, he said, 'She's been dead some time. We'll have to stay here.'

He tapped a number into his mobile.

'What can I do, sir?' Flora said.

'Ring Inspector Asquith, tell him what we've found here, give him my compliments and ask him if he will secure the scene ASAP. And ask him if we could have some men here right away.'

'Right, sir,' she said as she started tapping a number into her mobile.

Then into his mobile phone, Angel said, 'Don? ... How much longer will you be there? ... Oh, can you speed it up? ... we've just found the body of a woman ... I think it's Mr Piddington's carer ... very messy, certainly murder ... get over here as soon as you've finished everything there ... and would you tell Dr Mac?'

He gave Taylor the address and then rang off.

He looked up at Flora. She was still on the call to Inspector Asquith.

He tapped in another number. It was soon answered. 'Control room, Bromersley. Sergeant Clifton speaking.'

Angel told him what they had found, that it looked like murder and instructed him to inform Superintendent Harker immediately. Clifton said that he would. Then he said, 'And have you seen anything of Trevor Crisp?'

'No, sir,' Clifton said. 'Have you lost him again?'

'If you see him, Bernie, will you tell him that I'm looking for him? I'll get a dog collar and a lead and wrap that round his bloody neck if he doesn't stop disappearing like this, just when I need him. When he does turn up he'll have more apologies, explanations and justifications than Rupert Murdoch.'

'I'll put out a call for him, sir.'

'Thank you, Bernie.'

He rang off.

Flora closed her phone at the same time. She said, 'Inspector Asquith said he would put it on his list and that he will send four men straightaway. He said he will have to take them from traffic duty.'

'Right,' he said. 'If you're happy staying here on your own until help arrives, I'll start on the door to door.'

She stretched up to her best height, squared her shoulders and said, 'I'll be all right, sir.'

He nodded. She was very competent. He wasn't really in any doubt about it. 'All right,' he said. 'See if you can get Trevor Crisp on his mobile. I never can. If you can, tell him I want him here smartish.'

'Right, sir.'

Angel turned round and knocked on the door opposite. It had

the figure 20 painted crudely on it. There was no reply. He tried again, but no one answered. He moved along the corridor to number 23. That was the flat adjacent to Nancy Quinn's flat. There, an elderly woman holding a cat opened the door on the chain. She wouldn't let Angel in until she had had a close look at his police badge, photograph and name.

'You'd better come inside, Inspector Angel, and let me close the door so that I can put my little soldier down. If I let him out there's no knowing what those children will do to him.' She tickled the cat on the top of its head, put a hand under its stomach and lowered it to the ground. 'There you are,' she said. The cat meowed and ran behind the settee.

'Please sit down, Inspector Angel. Now, what is all this about?'

Angel looked round the pleasant little room, sat down on the settee and said, 'Firstly, may I ask you your name?'

'Mrs Vera Roman. I'm a widow.'

'I take it you live here alone?'

'Sadly, yes. When my husband died I didn't want to stay at our four-bedroom detached house on Creesford Road. There was such a lot of work running it, so I sold it and moved here in 1995. I used to be the manageress and buyer at the ladies' department at Avery's department store, and moving here was the biggest mistake of my life. Cyril, that's my late husband, Cyril would have been appalled. *Appalled* he would have been. *Absolutely appalled!*'

'I wonder if you could tell me about your next-door neighbour in number 21.'

'Who? Nancy? I don't know her very well, Inspector. Why, what's the matter? What's happened?'

'We are not sure. That's why I am asking you. There's been an incident that we are looking into. That's all I can say, at the moment.'

'Oh? An incident involving Nancy Quinn? I bet it involves a man. She's a nurse, isn't she? A very pretty girl. But I don't know her very well.'

Angel's eyebrows shot up. 'Nurse? Is she a professional nurse?'

'She *says* she is. I have my doubts. She's always scratching round for work, and I thought we were short of nurses. Tell you what, Inspector. She's not short of men. But they don't seem to last for long.'

'Has there been one lately? Say yesterday, last night?'

'Yes. A big fellow. Very nicely spoken. Handsome. Really nice. She doesn't usually seem to attract nice men like he was.'

Angel had a job concealing his excitement. 'You saw him yesterday?'

'It was yesterday morning, early. I was letting my cat in. He'd escaped and been out all night. Well, you know, I didn't expect my cat to be there. But he was. I opened the door, and he literally *fell* in. I was so relieved.'

'Tell me, what did you see of the man?'

'He was passing. I heard Nancy's flat door close and this big fellow passed about the time I opened my door and was picking up my cat. He said, "Good morning, my dear." I remember that.' She beamed. 'A woman my age doesn't forget a man who calls her "my dear" in such a nice way.'

'Where was he going?'

'Towards the lifts.'

'And what time was this, Mrs Roman? Can you remember?'

'Not exactly. I had only just woken up. Maybe seven or eight o'clock.'

'Does that mean he spent all night with her?'

'Probably. Come along, Inspector. It is 2013. All her boyfriends spend nights there, as far as I know.'

'And you didn't see him at all later on?'

'I haven't seen either of them since.'

'Do you know his name?'

'No. But why don't you ask her directly, yourself?'

'Can you hear anything through the wall?'

'No. Well I have heard the occasional shout or raised voice, when she's having a little row or something like that, I suppose. I mean … nobody's perfect, you know, Inspector.'

'No, indeed. And did you hear raised voices or shouting or banging doors anytime yesterday?'

'No,' she said. 'But why don't you ask her yourself?'

'And were you in all day yesterday?'

'I hardly ever go out. The supermarket and the shops round here deliver all I need for my cat and myself. Mrs Gamble's daughter, Eileen, will get me anything out of the ordinary that I might need.'

'Who is Mrs Gamble?'

'She's in number 24. Her door's opposite mine. Eileen is a lovely girl. And she's a good little shopper. Always knows where she can get it cheaper.'

Angel wrote the name Gamble down; having that would make it easier to open the conversation with the lady when he made his next port of call.

'Now, what do you know about Nancy Quinn's latest man? Can you describe him for me?'

Mrs Roman smiled. 'About your height, Inspector,' she said. 'Yes, tall, dark and handsome. He looks as if he could take care of himself in a fight. In fact, he's not unlike you. And a beautiful face. Like the face of a cherub. A real babyface.'

Angel's face muscles tightened. 'Me? A babyface?' he growled.

'Dear me, no. No,' she said quickly. 'You're not a bit similar in the face.'

He was relieved to hear it.

'Thank you,' he said, making a show of writing down what she was saying. 'All this information will help us, Mrs Roman.'

'What's happened? Are you after him? Is he wanted by the police? Why, what's he done?'

'We're not sure *he's* done anything, Mrs Roman. We need to speak to him to help us with our enquiries, that's all.'

She looked at Angel suspiciously. 'You've not told me why you're asking all these questions.'

'Please don't worry about it, Mrs Roman. There's been an incident next door. That's all. I'll tell you all about it at the right time. Now, what about his clothes? What was he wearing the last time you saw him … yesterday morning, wasn't it?'

'I have only ever seen him in a plain dark suit, black leather shoes, white shirt and blue tie.'

'Any peculiarities, mannerisms, speech impediments?'

'I don't think so. Well, we didn't have much contact. I only saw him twice … I think, but he had a beautiful speaking voice … like Richard Burton.'

Angel recalled Burton's voice. It certainly had many great attributes. 'Do you mean the man is Welsh?'

'Oh no,' she said. 'His voice has no accent that I could detect.'

'No accent, eh? That's interesting,' he said. 'Right, do you happen to know if Nancy Quinn is local? Does she ever talk to you about her family and friends? Does anybody ever visit her?'

'As I've said, a steady stream of men, that I saw. I shouldn't be saying things like that, should I? I never saw anybody who might be described as family, but I don't know they *weren't* family, do I?'

Angel stood up. 'Of course you don't. Don't worry about it. I think that's it, for now, Mrs Roman.'

'Oh, are you going, Inspector? And I never invited you to have a cup of tea.'

'That's all right. Thank you for your help. You stay where you are. I'll let myself out.'

'Wait while I get my cat, Inspector,' she said. 'If I don't pick him up, he'll be off like a shot.'

FOUR

As Angel closed the door of Mrs Roman's flat, DS Trevor Crisp, who had been chatting with DS Flora Carter outside Nancy Quinn's flat, saw him. He left Flora and rushed down the hall towards him.

Crisp knew he was potentially in trouble, but he wasn't going to let it show.

He smiled and said, 'Good morning, sir. I hear you want me.'

Angel glared at him. 'The morning's nearly over, lad. I've been trying to make contact with you since 8.30. Where the *hell* have you been?'

'I was delayed, sir.'

'*Delayed?*' Angel said. 'For *two* hours? It had better have been on very urgent business, lad.'

'It was on police business, sir,' he said with all the sincerity he could muster.

'Go on, then, lad. Spit it out. Tell me about it.'

Crisp licked his lips. 'I don't think you are in the mood to give me a fair hearing, sir.'

'I think you're probably right, but then again I've heard all sorts of half-baked excuses from you in the past; why would I expect this excuse to be any more reasonable?'

'There you are, sir. I *knew* you'd say something like that.'

Angel's eyes were like lasers and they were unswervingly focused on Crisp's.

'Get on with it!' Angel said.

Crisp ran the tip of his tongue along his bottom lip. He tried to look directly at Angel, but it was difficult. He didn't know quite where to look. 'Well, I went into that shop in Clement Attlee square on my way to the station, sir. Gregg's the newsagents.'

'Yes, lad,' Angel said. 'Well, get on with it. You've got my full attention. You wanted a copy of the *Beano*?'

'No, sir. I wanted a copy of the May issue of *Police Review*.'

'How very virtuous,' Angel said. 'And I bet he didn't have one.'

'No, sir, he didn't.'

Angel ran his hand through his hair and said, 'So what? Come on, lad. Get to the point.'

'Well, Mr Gregg began complaining about a white Ford transit van being parked outside his shop. He said that it had been there every day for the past two weeks. It arrived just before eleven o'clock in the morning and it was still there at eleven o'clock at night. And he said that its presence made deliveries difficult, and besides that, it put people off coming into his shop.'

'I don't see why it would. There's room for about eight vehicles to wait there, I believe. Anyway, Clement Attlee Square isn't in a restricted area, is it? The driver can park there all day, if he wants to.'

'Yes, sir. I know. And I told him that, but there's more to it than that.'

'Oh? If Gregg doesn't like the driver parking his van there all day, there's nothing he can legally do about it. You should have suggested that he had a friendly chat with the driver and tried to persuade him to park it somewhere else for a change.'

'That's exactly what I did say, sir, but he said he never sees anybody get out of the van, sir.'

'Well, he should hang about the van and catch the driver when he returns later in the day.'

'I said *that* to him as well, sir. But he insisted that he couldn't catch anybody returning at that time. He's a newsagent's, sir. He starts work at 5.30 a.m., so he has to go to bed early.'

Angel shook his head slowly several times. He sighed, then said, 'Well, we all have our problems, lad, and your problem is that you have to convince me that it took almost two and a half hours to explain the law to Mr Gregg and to direct him on the best course for him to take.'

'Well, customers kept coming into the shop. We kept being interrupted.'

'Is that it, then? Is that the best you can do?'

'Well, er yes, sir.'

Angel ran his hand through his hair, then he said, 'Well, it's a damned good job I'm busy and haven't time to bawl you out. As it is, I have *two* murders on my hands, and—'

'Yes, sir. Flora has been telling me.'

'What you don't know, you'll have to pick up as we go along. I've started the door to door. I found a badly battered female body in Flat 21, which I assume is that of Nancy Quinn. I also assume that she left old man Piddington at 7 p.m. last night and came back here. So she was assaulted and killed sometime after that. I want to know anything at all you can find out about her, her visitors, and her activities.'

'Right, sir,' Crisp said.

Angel heard footsteps from behind. He turned and saw two figures in white overalls, caps and wellington boots. They were Don Taylor and a PC from the SOCO team. They were standing outside the door of Flat 21 and were being greeted by Flora Carter.

Angel wanted to get to them.

He turned back to Crisp and said, 'I couldn't get a reply from Flat 22, but I've done 23 and 24. Carry on from there, lad.'

'Right, sir,' Crisp said. He turned away and began to look up at the numbers on the doors.

Angel dashed up the corridor. 'Hey, Don,' he said. 'Did you find any prints on old man Piddington's wheelchair?'

'Yes, sir. There are no prints on the handles at the back of the chair because the handgrips on the handles are ribbed rubber or imitation rubber. However, there are prints on the top rail at the back. I don't know yet whose they are, but I don't think they are necessarily indicative of any foul play; I mean, the owner of the prints could have been adjusting Mr Piddington's cushion or something. They are of a small hand ... could be Nancy Quinn's or Christine Elsworth's. Anyway, they are not Piddington's. We found his prints on the armrests and the handle of the security brake as you would expect.'

Angel nodded. 'Well, let me have a result on that ASAP. Did you find anything else?'

'No, sir. Not a thing.'

'Did Mac happen to say how long Piddington had been dead?'

'He said he'd been dead between ten and sixteen hours.'

'Mac saw him at about ten o'clock; that means he died between six o'clock and ten o'clock last night,' Angel said. He rubbed his chin. 'Has Mac had the body removed?'

'Yes, sir. The crime scene's all yours.'

Angel returned to 22 Jubilee Park Road with Flora Carter in the BMW. He was particularly eager to examine Mr Piddington's wheelchair.

It had been righted, appeared to be undamaged, and still had a light covering of aluminium dust on the smooth metal parts that SOCO had applied while looking for fingerprints.

He leaned over, grabbed the chair by the arms, picked it up and held it for a few seconds to feel the weight of it. It wasn't heavy, but it was awkward to hold in that position for any length of time. He lowered it back down onto the hall floor.

'Now then, Flora,' he said. 'Do you think you could pull this upstairs with a smallish man in the chair?'

'Can I try it first as it is, sir?'

'Of course.'

She went to the back of the chair and backed it up to the bottom step of the stairs, then, standing on the second step, she gripped the handles, and attempted to pull the chair backwards and upwards onto the first step. She couldn't quite manage it.

Angel, watching closely, said, 'Try putting a hand on the banister rail, and with the other, grip the metal cross bar in the centre of the back of the chair, and lift it from that position.'

It worked, and she progressed up the stairs, one at a time, and was at the top in a few seconds. It wasn't at all difficult.

'Now come on down, the same way,' Angel said.

When she reached the bottom, she smiled and said, 'How's that, sir?'

Angel nodded, and rubbing his chin he said, 'Now, do you think you could manage it with a ten-stone man in the chair?'

'I really don't know, sir. But I'd give it a try. Where are we going to find a ten-stone man?'

Angel opened his mobile and tapped in a number.

Ahmed answered. 'Yes, sir?'

'What do you weigh, lad?'

There was a slight pause before Ahmed said, 'Did you ask me what I weighed, sir?'

'Yes. In stones and pounds.'

Ahmed hesitated, then said, 'I weigh ten stone six, sir.'

'That's near enough. Come to 22 Jubilee Park Road rightaway. Who is the duty officer in the control room?'

'Sergeant Clifton, sir.'

'Right. Go up to the control room now and report to him.'

Angel switched the phone off, then on again and tapped out another number.

It was answered immediately. 'Control room, Bromersley Police Station, DS Clifton, duty officer.'

'It's Angel, Bernie. I urgently need PC Ahmed Ahaz here at the crime scene. I've told him to come directly to you. Will you find him some transport to bring him here ASAP?'

'Right, sir. Everything's out, but I'll find something.'

'Thank you, Bernie.'

He closed the phone and turned to Flora. 'He won't be long. Let's have a look around. Let's start upstairs.'

They went upstairs and found the two large bedrooms in a reasonably good state of repair and decoration. They had curtains at the windows, and rather worn but still serviceable fitted carpets, but there was no furniture. The bathroom was a bit dusty and had the unmistakable air of being used very little.

Angel came out onto the landing. He turned to Flora and said, 'I can't see any reason why old man Piddington would have wanted to come up here.'

'No, sir. Perhaps, latterly he never bothered. It's a big house for just one person.'

They went downstairs, where there was a small kitchen, sitting room and another room Mr Piddington had used as his bedroom. There was a lavatory off a tiny cloakroom which also had a washbasin and was clearly part of the original building that had been built about 1920, although the washbasin had been replaced by a much bigger bowl. A shower room had also been added, taking space from what had been a large pantry.

In the sitting room was a bureau. Angel opened it and busied himself looking through the various pigeonholes and small drawers, while Flora searched two chests of drawers, a bedside cabinet and a wardrobe in the bedroom.

She came into the sitting room. 'Nothing in there at all helpful, sir. Can I do anything in here?'

Angel looked up. 'No. There's nothing here either,' he said as he closed the bureau.

They heard the front door open and then close.

'Somebody's here,' Flora said.

Angel closed the bureau. 'It could be Ahmed,' he said.

They went out into the hall.

Ahmed was standing there looking around. He saw Angel.

'There you are, sir. Came as soon as I could.'

'Ah yes, Ahmed,' he said. 'I want to see if it's possible for DS Carter here to pull you up these stairs in that wheelchair.'

Angel looked at Flora with eyebrows raised.

She nodded in agreement, then turned to Ahmed, smiled and said, 'Only if you agree, Ahmed?'

Angel said, 'I'll stand in front of you, lad, and follow you up. If she falters, can't do it or lets go of the chair, I'll be there to stop you and the chair rolling down to the bottom. All right? It's not a game or to settle a bet or anything like that, Ahmed. It's solely in the interest of bringing a murderer to justice.'

'Oh yes, sir,' Ahmed said. 'I don't mind.'

He could hardly resist Flora's beautiful smile, plus the promise of support from a man he thought could do no wrong.

Angel pushed the back wheels of the wheelchair against the rise of the bottom step, looked at Ahmed and pointed to the seat. Ahmed got into the chair and held onto the padded black arms. Flora squeezed past the newel post, took up her position on the stairs, put an arm down the back of the chair and gripped the tubular frame. She put the other hand out to the handrail of the banisters.

Angel stood facing Ahmed. 'Right, lad, now you just sit there and keep hold of the armrests. All right?'

Ahmed looked as cool as prison milk. 'Right, sir,' he said.

Angel looked up at Flora. 'Now, lass,' he said. 'In your own time, see if you can pull him up to the top. If you can't, don't hurt yourself, just let go.'

Flora Carter gripped the framework of the chair tightly and pushing on the handrail proceeded to try to lift the chair with Ahmed in the seat up to the first step. She raised him three inches, then hesitated, then continued upward until the back wheels rested on the first step. Angel closed up. She repeated the pull and arrived on the second step. After that the momentum increased and she soon reached the top step and then the landing. Angel closed up only inches away from the chair at any time. She pulled the wheelchair safely away from the top of the stairs, then looked at Angel, who was beaming. 'Well done, Flora,' he said.

She then looked at Ahmed and said, 'Are you all right?'

Ahmed beamed. 'Yes, thank you, Sarge.'

'Well, so far so good,' Angel said. 'We now know that Nancy Quinn *could* have dragged that chair with Mr Piddington in it up these stairs.'

'Yes, sir, and if she had murdered him, have you discovered a motive?'

'Not yet. But she seems the most likely. There's a lot more work to do on this. Look, Flora, find out who Mr Piddington's GP is from Christine Elsworth, see him and ask him if it would have been possible for the old man to have dragged his wheelchair up these stairs himself.'

'Right, sir,' she said.

'And you can drop Ahmed off back at the station on your way.'

'Right, sir,' she said. 'Come on, Ahmed.'

Flora and Ahmed ran down the stairs and out of the front door.

When they had gone, Angel sat in the wheelchair and ran it along the landing into an empty bedroom to get used to the feel of it. Then he ran it back along the landing to the top of the stairs and looked down. He could see that it would be frightening to anyone unable to walk and dependent on a wheelchair for mobility. After a moment or two, he wheeled the chair carefully forward up to the edge of the step, then, while holding onto the banister rail with one hand, he rolled forward so that the front wheels of the chair ran over the edge of the step. The wheelchair promptly bounced uncomfortably downwards twenty or thirty inches, then stopped abruptly at a precarious angle. The front wheels were suspended more than an inch above the next step down, and the wheelchair refused to move downwards any further. The front wheels were very much smaller in diameter than the back wheels.

Angel released his grip of the banister rail and tried to wheel the chair backward, but even his strength could not return it any distance. He then tried to wheel the chair forward, but it would not budge. He realized that it would definitely have needed somebody to tilt the chair back by holding down the handles to allow the chair with its passenger to run dangerously down to the bottom. Of course, Mr Piddington could easily have fallen forward out of the chair and down the steps with the same end result, but the evidence was that he came down *with* the chair. Angel was now satisfied, nay positive, that he was investigating a case of murder.

He got out of the chair, squeezed past it and wheeled it down the stairs to the hall.

He was anxious to see what Dr Mac had discovered from the body of Nancy Quinn when his mobile phone rang.

He pulled it out of his pocket, glanced at the LCD screen, saw that it was the superintendent, wrinkled his nose, pressed the button and said, 'Angel. Yes, sir?'

'Now then, lad,' Harker said. 'How are you getting on with that triple nine?'

'It's a murder case, sir. And it has led us to another body in Commodore House. Everything is going to plan. Still at the stage of gathering evidence, interviewing witnesses, awaiting forensic reports and—'

'Aye well, you'll have to break off that. I've had a worrying call from the manager of the Royal Westminster Bank, Mr Ballantyne. I don't know what it's about. He couldn't discuss it over the phone, he said. You know what banks are like for secrecy. He wanted me to go and see him ASAP. Well, I can't go. I'm up to my neck in finalizing the details of this meeting of ACPO here in July. I told him I'd have to send you. See what is troubling him and sort it out … you'll know what to say. I bank there so I don't want him upsetting. All right?'

Angel wasn't pleased. 'Well, I've two murders on my hands, sir. Time just now is at a premium. Perhaps you could send—'

'Don't be difficult, Angel,' Harker bawled. 'Rodney Ballantyne is a very important man. It is imperative that we keep good relations with key people in the town. I told him you'd see him within the hour. Ask for his secretary and tell her you're expected. Now get on with it.'

There was a click and the phone went dead.

Angel was furious. But it was useless arguing. He'd never heard of Rodney Ballantyne and he couldn't care less about the Royal Westminster Bank. He was never likely to be interested in the manager of the bank unless a serious crime was threatened or had already been committed. He doubted that that was the situation. And he had two serious crimes to deal with already. No crime was more serious than murder.

He stormed outside, ignored the constable on the door, got into his car, started the engine, rammed the gearstick into first gear and let in the clutch.

FIVE

'I'm Rodney Ballantyne, pleased to meet you, Inspector Angel. Please sit down. Tell me, that name is familiar. I wonder … are you the same Inspector Angel I read about from time to time who always gets his man, like the Canadian Mounted Police?'

Angel sat down and looked at the man across the desk. 'It's often reported like that,' he said.

'You mean you *don't* always get your man?' Ballantyne asked.

Angel wished he had simply said, 'Yes.'

'Well,' he said, 'it really only applies to cases of murder. It *is* true to say that, with a lot of help from my team and sometimes some very sophisticated forensics, the investigations of the murder cases I've been involved with have been successful; the murderer has been caught, tried and sentenced. But there's always a first time, when I might not be so lucky, and I don't want to tempt providence. Now, Mr Ballantyne, I am sure that your problem is nothing to do with murder.'

'No. It certainly isn't, but it's worrying nevertheless.'

He opened the middle drawer of his desk and took out six £5 notes in an elastic band. He whisked off the elastic and dealt them out like playing cards in front of Angel.

'Please have a look at them, Inspector,' Ballantyne said.

Angel picked one up, looked at it, turned it over, looked at it and then put it down. It was clean and crisp and hardly handled.

'They're not forgeries, are they? They're very good if they are.'

'No. They're not forgeries. They were stolen from this bank thirty years ago. And they turned up in the cash paid in last Friday. They were put through our counting machine which rejected them because they are, strictly speaking, no longer valid currency. This issue was withdrawn in 1998. These six £5 notes are from a consignment of freshly minted notes, which were stolen from this branch in 1983. I've been in touch with our bank's local director in York. He says that three men raided the bank in 1983 and got away with more than ten million pounds in £20, £10 and £5 denominations, straight from the mint. The men had handguns, and wore Yogi Bear masks. Two men were eventually caught and were given ten years' imprisonment. The third man was never found.'

'Did the bank recover any of the money?'

'No. And none of the notes had been paid into this branch until last Friday when those six notes turned up. Of course, I can't speak for other banks or other branches of this bank.'

'And have you any idea who paid them in?'

Ballantyne shook his head. 'We know it was one of about 750 depositors.'

It was Angel's turn to shake his head. 'You can't possibly whittle it down?'

'I'm afraid not. Friday is a busy day, and we can't have customers waiting more than a minute or so at the counters. We also have the additional complication of the need for cashiers to exchange denominations between themselves, from time to time.'

Angel wrinkled his nose. He rubbed his chin. 'Well, how many times would the cashiers need to do that in the course of a day?'

'I don't know. I never thought. It all depends on how much cash is paid in, and in what denominations, and alternatively if there is the need to pay a lot of cash out, and again, in what denominations. It's impossible to say.'

'Well, put a figure on it.'

Ballantyne shrugged, then said, 'Up to fifteen times perhaps.' Then he added, 'It *might* be possible for us to install a system that records each exchange, although it would mean an extra internal transaction. That would be very time-consuming.'

'To be effective, each teller would have to record each note by its number?'

'Dear me. I suppose so. Couldn't do that, Inspector. It would take *far* too long.'

Angel nodded. He understood perfectly.

He had thought of something else. 'Anyway, what would prevent your tellers from re-issuing the notes to a customer who wants to withdraw cash from their account?'

'Nothing at all. Unless the teller happened to notice that the picture of Her Majesty was not the current one. But that's a lot to expect when large sums are being paid in and there is a queue of half a dozen busy and impatient customers to serve.'

'Seems to me,' Angel said, running his hand across his mouth, 'that the only certain way of identifying the depositor of the old notes would be at the time the deposit was being made.'

'You are absolutely right, Inspector, but I'm not sure that I can expect our tellers to be as observant as that.'

'Well, I think you will have to make them aware of the situation, Mr Ballantyne, otherwise there may not be much hope of identifying the person who deposited them.'

'You're right, of course,' he said. 'I will try and get their cooperation. It may be a good idea to stick one of these six notes at each till, right in front of their noses, to remind them that they're now in circulation.'

Angel nodded in agreement, then said, 'What has happened to the robbers?'

'I don't know. I was told that they pleaded their innocence at the time of their arrest, throughout the trial and when they were in prison.'

Angel blinked. That was a surprise. 'And the third man?' he said.

'He was never identified.'

Angel pursed his lips and his eyes narrowed.

Angel came out of the Royal Westminster Bank and got into the BMW. As he was putting his key into the ignition, his mobile rang out. He glanced at the screen. The caller was the Chief Constable. Angel's eyebrows shot up. This *was* unusual. Contact with the boss was rare and was usually about matters of discipline or special commendation, and as he was not aware that he was up for either, he couldn't guess what he wanted. He pressed the key and said, 'Angel. Yes, sir?'

It was a woman who spoke. 'Good afternoon, Detective Inspector. It's Mrs Murchison. How are you?'

She was the Chief's secretary. Angel had hardly spoken to her over the six or seven years she had been in the job, but they knew each other by sight well enough. However, he couldn't imagine what she wanted.

'I am fine, thank you, Mrs Murchison,' he said in his best Sunday voice. 'And I trust you are well?'

'I am very well, thank you. Now, the Chief Constable wants you to make yourself available for a short meeting in his office tomorrow morning at nine o'clock. He wants to address all senior officers, so Superintendent Harker and Inspector Asquith will also be present. That's all.'

Angel wondered what it was about. Maybe the Chief was moving on, retiring or being promoted. He didn't think so. Or perhaps there was to be another Home Office inspection. He hoped not.

'Is that all right, Inspector?' she added.

'Yes, of course. I will be there, Mrs Murchison. Thank you.'

'Goodbye, Inspector Angel.'

'Goodbye, Mrs Murchison.'

He closed the phone. His first thought was to ring Haydn Asquith, the uniformed inspector, and the only other inspector at the station, to see if he knew what the meeting was about, but he decided against it. The meeting was early the next morning. He would have to control his curiosity until then. He pocketed the phone and started the BMW. He looked at the time on the dashboard. It said 16.22 hours.

He couldn't make his mind up where to go next. He wanted to see what SOCO had turned up at each of the crime scenes. That was important. Trevor Crisp was on the door to door, he might have some useful information. That was important too. Flora Carter was seeing Piddington's GP to find out about his health and his capabilities. That would certainly be very useful. And then there was Dr Mac, who might have conclusive information about the cause of death of both the old man and his carer and maybe other information that modern science can sometimes determine from dead bodies.

He decided to visit Dr Mac. The mortuary was on the right side of town to leave him well placed to get home at a reasonable time for once.

He duly arrived at Bromersley District General Hospital, found a car park space, went into the hospital, and made his way up the long corridor to the mortuary. The door was always locked as it had been known for bodies to go missing. He rang the bell and an assistant in a green overall recognized him, admitted him and told him that Dr Mac was in his office at the far end of the department.

The mortuary was a big, smelly suite of rooms, white tiled, and with huge windows. Gutters, green hosepipes and banks of refrigerated bodies stood on the side and there was water, water everywhere. There was a constant smell of ammonia, sulphurated hydrogen and carbolic soap.

As he passed through the theatre, there was a body on an operating table covered with a green cloth.

Angel reached the offices.

Mac looked up from his writing through the internal window of his office and saw Angel approaching. He smiled and waved him in.

'I thought you wouldn't be far away,' Mac said, as he pointed to a chair. 'Sit down.'

Angel looked round the little office, although he had been there many times before. 'I don't know how you work in this abominable smell,' he said as he closed the door and eased himself into the chair.

'You get used to it. You've timed it well. I've just finished the examination of the young woman. I haven't written it up yet, but I should be able to email it to you tomorrow.'

'That's great, Mac. Just give me the basic info I need to know.'

'Well, I can confirm that the body is that of Nancy Quinn. She's been a patient at this hospital, so I've been able to get her records. She was born on 11 October 1988. Admitted three years ago for appendicitis, and she has the scar to prove it. Also, in 1992 she had a mastoidectomy, which also left her with a scar behind the right ear. So it all checks out. She died from eighteen stab wounds to the neck, chest, back, stomach and thighs. The weapon was a thin knife with a blade at least six inches long. Could have been an ordinary steak knife.'

The corners of Angel's mouth turned down, and he recalled the image he saw when he entered her poky flat in Commodore House.

Mac said, 'And there's something else, Michael. And you won't like this either.'

Angel frowned. 'What's that?'

'She was beaten, I would say systematically, on several occasions.'

'On *several* occasions?'

'Two or three times. There are contusions all over her stomach, buttocks, chest, thighs and her arms. They seem to have been inflicted with a clenched fist. The skin wasn't punctured and none of the contusions were on her hands or her face. The varying condition of the skin indicates that they were inflicted over a period of time … on different occasions … say, over ten days or two weeks or so.'

Angel wrinkled his nose and shook his head.

'What some people have to tolerate. Was the weapon – the steak knife – found?'

'I haven't seen it. Don Taylor didn't mention it. There might be more when the analyses of the stomach contents, the liver and so on come back from the lab. No visual signs of drugs or foreign substances.'

'Any needle marks?'

'Couldn't find any.'

Angel considered all that Mac had told him and then said, 'Have you finished your examination of the old man?'

'Yes. Except for the writing up. He broke his neck, which snapped his spine and he died instantly.'

The muscles in Angel's face tightened. 'It's a relief to know that he died straightaway. Any other wounds?'

'Bruising of his hands, fingers and his right elbow, no doubt incurred trying to save himself as he fell.'

'Those wounds couldn't have been inflicted while defending himself against an attack by somebody?'

'They could have, but it is usually the case that when we are falling we put out our open hands in front of us to try to limit the impact of a fall, or to find something to grab hold of to save ourselves. It may not be a brilliant idea, Michael, but that's the reflex action most people take if they find themselves falling forward.'

'I'm sure you're right, Mac. Just looking at all the options.'

It was 5.15 p.m.

Angel drove the BMW straight into the open garage, pulled down the door, locked it, walked along the path to the back of his house, unlocked the kitchen door, went in and closed the door. He looked round. There was no sign of Mary.

'Anybody home?' he called. 'Hello. Is there anybody there?'

But there was silence. She did not reply.

However, there were the giveaway signs that food was being prepared: the warmth from the oven, the smell of cooking meat, and the sight of pots and kitchen utensils soaking in the sink.

He bent down and looked through the glass door of the oven and saw a casserole dish. He nodded with satisfaction and anticipation.

He went through the kitchen into the hall and called up the stairs. 'Anybody home? I'm back.'

'Hello, darling,' Mary called. 'I'm in the loft. I'm coming down now.'

His eyebrows shot up. He wondered why she was in the loft. There was nothing up there but a thick layer of dust, a thicker wadding of insulation, cardboard boxes of rubbish and a lagged water tank.

'No rush, love,' he called. 'Any post?'

'On the hall table,' she said smartly. 'It's *always* on the hall table.'

'Aye,' he said quietly, then shook his head. He was thinking, he knew it was *always* on the hall table except when it *wasn't*, which was three or four times a week. Then it was on the worktop in the kitchen, or in Mary's handbag or on the mantelshelf or somewhere totally impossible to guess such as tucked inside her library book.

He glanced down at the hall table. There was one envelope. He knew the sender before he picked it up. He wrinkled his nose. It was from the gas company, a cheap brown window envelope, in an irregular size. He tore it open. It was never good news. Either the price of gas was going up, or he was behind with the payments. He read it quickly. There were four long paragraphs of reasons, excuses, explanations and glorification of the company and the wisdom of the directors followed by the hard news that the cost of gas was being increased by five per cent a therm in a month's time. Angel frowned. Five per cent a therm? What does that mean in money? By how much is it going to increase the cost of the bill? The letter didn't say. He was mulling over the possible consequences of the increase in price, when Mary appeared.

'You're early, love, is everything all right?'

'Yes, fine. What you doing in the attic?'

She saw him holding the letter. 'What's that?'

'Letter from the gas company. They're shoving the price of gas up again.'

'Oh. I was looking for an atlas. I thought we had an atlas. A big flat book with a blue cover.'

'I know what it looks like,' he said. 'You put it in the church jumble. You said it was out of date.'

Her jaw dropped. 'So *that's* where it went. Of course I did. I remember now. No wonder I couldn't find it. We need an up-to-date one. Anyway, what's the capital of Ethiopia?'

'Addis Ababa. Well, don't dash out and get one. Don't buy anything we can manage without, for goodness sake.'

'Addis Ababa. Of course it is,' she said, sounding relieved. 'We *do* need an atlas, Michael. Everybody needs an atlas.'

'I don't and you don't. We can't eat it, we can't wear it and it'll not help to keep us warm next winter. If you need to know anything about the world, you can go to the library or look it up on the Internet. Anyway, what do you want to know the capital of Ethiopia for?'

'It's for a competition.'

He wrinkled his nose. 'Not *another* competition? You'll never win anything. Nobody ever does. It's not worth the postage.'

Her face went scarlet. 'I know. *I know*,' she said. 'You gave me a lecture on the cost of stamps yesterday.'

'Well, as I said, we've got to watch our costs, Mary,' he said.

She didn't reply, just breathed in and out very loudly, then turned away.

Angel was utterly exasperated. She was always annoyed whenever he tried to talk about making savings. He stormed off to the sitting room. He put the television on and tried to become interested in it until she called him back into the kitchen for his tea. It wasn't until after the meal that their relationship returned to normal.

Angel put his dessert spoon and fork together and said, 'That was scrumptious, Mary love. Thank you.'

She smiled. 'I'll make the coffee and bring it through.'

He got up. 'Anything on the telly?' he said as he pushed his chair back to the table.

'They're re-running some episodes of *Bad Girls*,' she said. 'I recorded one this morning.'

His face lit up. 'I'll find it and set it up.' He made for the hall, then turned back. 'By the way, you remember that new white shirt you got for me. Have you had time to wash it?'

She turned away from filling the coffee pot and said, 'Did it yesterday. It's in the drawer, why?'

'Good. Got to see the Chief tomorrow at nine o'clock.'

'Oh? What've you been up to?'

He grinned. 'Nothing like that. I don't know what it's about. Just for officers.'

Mary pulled a face and said, 'Something important.'

SIX

It was 8.28 a.m. when Angel reached his office that Tuesday morning. He had his new shirt on and a different tie. It wasn't new although it looked new. It was one that his father used to wear on special occasions. His mother had given it to him years ago. Mary pointed out to her husband that the one he usually wore was becoming very slightly frayed where the knot was tied. He didn't want to make the change. He had got rather used to it. He had solved many difficult cases while wearing that tie, but he wanted to look his best for the Chief Constable.

He reached out for the phone and tapped in a number. It was soon answered by Ahmed. 'Good morning, sir.'

'Ahmed, I have an appointment with the Chief at nine. I don't expect it will take long. Tell DS Taylor I want to see him as soon as possible after that, I want to know how far he's got with the crime scene at Nancy Quinn's. Also find DS Crisp and tell him I want to see him ASAP. I want his report on the house to house. All right?'

'Yes, sir.'

He replaced the phone and was fingering through the post when there was a knock at the door.

'Come in.'

It was Flora. 'Good morning, sir.'

'Yes, Flora. I was going to give you a buzz. What did you find out?'

'Well, sir, Mr Piddington's GP said that in his judgement he would not have been able to mount the stairs. He had not been able to walk for more than three years. He had very little muscle remaining in his legs and he would have lost the rhythm and balance of climbing. He also said that he certainly would not have been able to drag a wheelchair up the stairs.'

Angel nodded. 'You make him sound very decisive.'

'He was, sir.'

'Then that confirms our theory that Piddington was murdered by Nancy Quinn or some other person.'

The phone rang. He pulled an impatient face and reached out for it.

'Angel.'

It was Superintendent Harker. 'Ah yes, Angel,' he said. 'Now, the Chief Constable will not be able to hold that meeting planned for this morning. Instead he has briefed me to convey the essence of what it is about, to you and Inspector Asquith, so come on up now to my office and let's get on with it.'

Angel frowned as he replaced the phone. He needn't have put his best shirt on if he had known. He looked across at Flora as he stood up. 'I've got a meeting with the super and DI Asquith now. In the meantime, find out all you can about Nancy Quinn. Start with our records, obviously, but then see what you can learn from HMRC, and so on. Got to go.'

'All right, sir,' Flora said.

Angel dashed out of the room and made straight up the corridor. As he reached the super's door, DI Haydn Asquith also arrived from the opposite direction. He was in his best uniform. His buttons had been polished so much that when they caught the light, they were dazzling.

'Ah, Michael. Any idea what this is about?' Asquith said.

'No,' he said. 'I thought we were to see the Chief.'

'We were. But last night he was offered a ticket to the big golf tournament at Turnberry. All the big world-class names will be there. He'll be on the plane now to Prestwick. Should be at Turnberry for ten o'clock when they tee off.'

Angel blinked. 'Really?'

'Yes. Who else is coming?'

'I understand it's just you and me, Haydn. We'd better go in.'

Angel knocked on the door and pushed it open. The smell of menthol hit him in the face like a hot towel.

Harker looked up from his desk. 'Sit down, lads. This won't take long. The Chief sends his apologies, but something extremely important cropped up at the last minute.'

Angel and Asquith exchanged glances, but avoided smiling as they turned to find chairs and sit down.

Harker coughed several times and turned over a mountain of paper from one side of his desk to the other, apparently searching for something. Eventually he spotted a thin file and pulled it out. 'Ah,' he said triumphantly.

He opened it and began to read, then he looked up and said, 'Yes. Now, this is very important and absolutely confidential, lads. You'll see why as I go along. It is a notification from ACPO, about a case referred to only as case number 1066 for security purposes. This is an ongoing case where two men knocked on the house door of a bank manager and his wife late at night, gained admittance, then pulled out handguns and threatened to kill the wife if the man didn't do as he was told. Very alarming stuff. The two villains stayed in the house overnight and the bank manager was instructed the next day to behave normally in every respect except that he was to assist in a robbery. The bank manager was told that a van would arrive at the rear door of the bank at noon and that he was to facilitate the other three members of the gang, enabling them to empty the bank vault and load it into the van. He was told that if anything went wrong, his wife would be decapitated. Imagine that? Decapitated!

'Anyway,' Harker continued, 'the bank manager duly left for work as usual unescorted, but with the fear of God pumped into him about what would happen to his wife if the job went wrong. Accordingly, the robbery took place and the gang got away with seven million pounds.

'The gang were rounded up, however, thanks to a quick-witted member of the bank staff who, suspecting that the manager was behaving oddly, rang up the local station and spoke to the head of the CID, who expertly followed the van to a farmhouse out in the sticks, then returned to the station. Later the CID and uniformed, supported by an Armed Response Unit, surrounded the farmhouse and arrested and charged the gang of five without a round being fired. The gang are obviously well disciplined and are saying, "No comment" to all questions, which I find alarming. Although this kidnapping and robbery involved five men, there may have been more.

'Now, the bank manager had obeyed the gang in every particular in the expectation that his wife would be at his house safe and sound. Instead she was not found until twenty-four hours later, six miles away, in an empty flat, tied up, rolled in a carpet, barely alive and out of her mind. For security reasons, her identity has been changed and she was transferred to a hospital in another part of the country. She is still ill and being treated for anxiety neurosis. She might never totally recover.'

Angel's facial muscles tightened as he considered the distress the couple must be enduring at that time, especially the manager's wife.

Harker continued: 'The Chief Constable doesn't want a repetition of this on this patch. He recognizes the power of gangs. It is reminiscent of Chicago in the twenties, and London in the sixties. A gang has to have a leader and if he can establish a controlling fear culture over a handful of men, and so rely on each of them to carry out his orders, and if each of the five could wield similar power over say, another five men, the man at the top would be mightily powerful.

'The position that *that* bank manager found himself in could happen to the Chief, me or either of you. It could happen to any senior policeman, bank official, judge, politician or anyone who has control over large sums of cash or is in a position to change the course of events to favour an organized gang of villains.

'So, the Chief wants to know if either of you have any notion of a gang of, say, four or more crooks, working in and about our patch.'

Harker looked up from the paper. 'Well?'

'There are none I can think of, sir,' Angel said.

'No, sir,' Asquith said.

'Well, if any come to light,' Harker said, 'report them to me. I know that the Chief has access to special funds he can call on from the Home Office to finance long-term surveillance, also sound-enhancing equipment and specialized officers to combat any such extreme situations. Right, lads, that's it. Any questions?'

Angel said, 'Yes sir, do you know how the bank manager's wife is now?'

Harker's face creased. He wasn't pleased. 'I've no idea, lad,' he said slowly and deliberately. 'This isn't a time for hearts and flowers. The point is, the Chief wants to know if there are any gangs on our patch, because if there are, he will introduce a programme to move them out. That's all.'

Angel returned to his office. He reached out for the phone and tapped in a number. It was soon answered.

Ahmed said, 'I made those phone calls, sir. DS Crisp is on his way from Commodore House. He should be here in five or ten minutes. And DS Taylor said he would come ASAP. He should be with you now.'

'Well, he isn't,' Angel said.

There was a knock at the door.

'That's probably him,' Angel said. 'Come in,' he called.

The door opened and it was DS Taylor. He was carrying a red paper file.

Angel slammed down the phone and turned to the sergeant. 'I expected you to be *here*.'

'Sorry, sir. I came as soon as I could. I assumed you wanted as much info as I could gather.'

'Your assumption was right. Well, sit down and tell me first if you've anything fresh on Piddington.'

'Only that those prints on the back of the wheelchair have still not been identified. He must have had some other person visiting him and I can only suppose that whoever it was tried to make him more comfortable by rearranging the cushions.'

Angel's face hardened. 'Or by pulling him to the top of the stairs and then letting go.'

Taylor looked at Angel a few moments before saying, 'I suppose it could have happened like that, sir. Shall I go on?'

Angel nodded.

'His prescription medicines appeared to be in order and in the appropriate quantities,' Taylor said. 'We have found fibres from the carpet at Piddington's sitting room on the sofa at Commodore House, but that's not at all surprising, as Nancy Quinn had been visiting the place twice a day.'

Angel nodded in agreement.

'There was no other forensic there, sir,' Taylor added.

There was no disguising Angel's disappointment. He pulled a face, sighed and then said, 'Right, Don. Now, what about Nancy Quinn's flat?'

Taylor said, 'Well, as you know, sir, the body was on a carpet on the floor. They may have been down there making love. Anyway, I believe that the first knife wound was delivered while they were on the carpet, because there was a spray of blood on the skirting board. The other thirteen wounds were delivered quickly afterward while she was still on the floor. There were two separate hairs, that are not hers, that we found on her. One on her neck and the other on her vest. It looked to me as if there had been a fair amount of sexual activity, maybe intercourse, taking place before or even during the stabbing. The wounds were made with a knife just about everywhere on her torso. She was dressed except for her tights, which were on the floor nearby. They were snagged in several places, so I suspect that they were probably removed by the man whilst still holding the knife.'

'You mean she was raped?'

'It could have been like that, or it could have been some sort of a sex game. You know how things are today, sir?'

Angel looked at him, blinked and then frowned.

Taylor looked at him in surprise, his eyebrows raised.

Angel said, 'What else did you find?'

Taylor hesitated. He looked down and shook his head. 'It's difficult to er ... show you this, sir,' Taylor said, fiddling with the red paper file he had brought with him.

Angel shook his head impatiently. 'Difficult? Difficult? What are you saying? What is it, man?'

Taylor looked down to avoid Angel's gaze, opened the red file he was still holding, bursting with photographs, took out the top one and held it out in his general direction. Angel grabbed it, turned it over and looked at it. It was a photograph of part of a bedroom showing a big area of the wall with red hieroglyphics scrawled over it. At the bottom of the photograph was part of a bed covered in women's clothes, mostly dresses, and on the right, part of a wardrobe with the door hanging open overflowing with clothes.

Angel gawped at the photograph, then quickly yanked open the top drawer of his desk and fished around for a hand magnifying glass. He put it over the red scrawl and slowly read it aloud, as he was able to make sense of it. '"Inspector A – don't get in my way."' He said it again.

His jaw dropped and his mouth fell open for a few seconds, then he gritted his teeth and said, 'Huh. He'd better not get in my way, whoever he is.'

Taylor looked up and said, 'You must know him, sir.'

Angel rubbed his chin. 'Hmm. Well, he doesn't come to mind.'

'Well, he knows you.'

Angel turned the photo over. It read: 'Nancy Quinn's No. 1 Bedroom. Flat 21, Commodore House. 12.55 hours. 6 May 2013.'

Taylor said, 'He used the corner of a nightdress of hers … soaked in blood … to daub that message on the wall.'

Angel looked grim. 'This is a threat, Don,' he said. 'This man is evil. He shows contempt for the law, and he doesn't value human life. We've got to catch him ASAP before he murders anybody else.'

'If you have any suspects in mind, sir, he'll have bloodstains on his clothes, trace evidence down his fingernails and on his shoes. If there's anybody we can pick up now—'

'There's nobody, Don. I have nothing yet to go on. Have you anything else?'

'Not at the moment, but we haven't finished. I still have four PCs working at Commodore House. Two are going through the mountain of clothes, vacuuming down garment by garment. And the other two are systematically searching the flat. Also I have her mobile phone. I'll be sifting through her calls. She didn't have a landline. We might still get something useful.'

'Right, Don. Crack on with it.'

Taylor stood up. He handed Angel the red file. 'These are all the pics of both the Piddington scene and the Nancy Quinn scene, sir.'

'Right, lad.'

Taylor went out.

Angel picked up the photograph of the message on the bedroom wall and stared at it, his nose turned upward as if he had accidentally smelled the gravy in the cookhouse at Strangeways.

He read the daubed message again. 'Inspector A – don't get in my way.' He said it aloud, then blinked several times. He wondered whom he knew or had known who might have murdered Nancy Quinn. It could have been a villain he had known or even locked up from the past. It could have been one of a thousand ... or even ten thousand.

There was a knock at the door.

Angel put the photograph in the red file, and said, 'Come in.'

It was Crisp. 'You wanted me, sir. I came as soon as I could.'

Angel pointed to a chair. 'Sit down, lad. Tell me, have you finished the door to door?'

'I've interviewed everybody on that floor except the ones you had done, sir. I took a photograph of her with me. None of them knew Nancy Quinn by sight or at all except the man in the flat opposite hers, number 22. A man called Raymond Rich, aged about thirty, lives on his own, works as a draughtsman at a factory in Sheffield during the day and at nights he's a DJ at "Lola's" nightclub. He said he'd seen several different men over the months come out of her flat when he returned from his gigs at one or two o'clock in the morning. He also said he thought she was very pretty. He had been out with her himself, but the relationship didn't last long.'

'Did he say why?'

'He said they just didn't click, sir. That was *his* word.'

Angel sniffed. 'Did he say he'd seen anybody in particular in the last week or so?' he said.

'Yes, sir. I was coming to that. Rich said that on Sunday morning last he saw a man let himself into her flat at about ten o'clock with a newspaper and a bottle of milk.'

Angel's face brightened. 'Let himself in?'

'Yes, sir. With a key.'

'Could he describe him?'

'Tall, black hair, athletic and young looking.'

'Young looking? What did he mean exactly?'

Crisp screwed up his face. 'Not sure, sir.'

Angel blew out a yard of air, then said, 'Well, you'd better go and find out. That man is very possibly her murderer! And I need the best possible description of the man you can get. Wake up, lad. And find out if they spoke. If it was only, "Good morning" he might have given his accent away or he might even have had a speech impediment.'

Crisp stood up. 'Raymond Rich will be at work now, sir,' he said. 'He works at Beasley's Foundries in Sheffield.'

'I don't care where he works, just find out as much as you can. And you'd better phone me when you get a result. Anything at all. Best ring on my mobile. I don't know quite where I'll be. I'm going out imminently to see Piddington's daughter.'

SEVEN

The delightful smell of the multicoloured blooms in the little flower kiosk just off the busy main road in the centre of Bromersley greeted Angel as he went through the open door. He glanced round. There was only a young girl at the small counter.

'Can I see Mrs Elsworth, please,' he said.

The girl peered round a doorway behind her and said, 'There's a man asking to see you, Christine.'

A second later Christine Elsworth appeared wearing a navy blue overall. She didn't look pleased when she saw it was Angel.

'Oh, it's you, Inspector.'

'Yes, Mrs Elsworth,' he said. 'Can we go somewhere quiet and talk?'

She nodded. 'Come in the back. It's not very big, I'm afraid.'

'That's all right,' he said.

He followed her behind the counter, through the doorway and into the small back room. The little room had had its door removed to make more space. It had a workbench, two stools, stacks of boxes, rolls of wrapping paper and twenty or so varieties of flowers in green tin vases of water standing on the floor. There was a strong smell of fresh greenery. On the bench was a metal tray in the shape of a cross. It was filled with wet oasis cut to fit and partly decorated with small red rosebuds. Angel looked at it curiously.

'I was busy with that,' she said as she sprayed the rosebuds with a fine mist of water. 'But it's all right. It'll keep. It's not wanted until two o'clock.'

In the background, Angel could still hear the murmur of dialogue between customers coming into the shop and the young assistant's softer and even quieter replies. It was cramped, but Angel had interviewed people in much worse conditions.

Christine Elsworth pointed to one of the stools. She put the spray on a shelf under the bench and sat on the other stool.

'I expected to hear from you yesterday,' she said.

Angel sat on the stool. He licked his lower lip. 'Yes. Sorry about that. It was an exceptionally busy day.'

She raised her eyebrows.

He thought she must not have heard about the murder of her father's carer.

'I went to interview Nancy Quinn and regrettably found her dead,' he said. 'She had been murdered.'

Christine Elsworth's face changed. Her jaw fell and her mouth dropped open. 'How awful,' she said. After a few moments she said, 'It makes me ashamed, Inspector.'

'Ashamed?' he said.

'I thought that she might have murdered my father.'

'We're still looking into that.'

Christine Elsworth shook her head.

'I have a few questions I must ask you,' he said.

She nodded.

'Who benefits from the death of your father?'

She frowned. 'I wouldn't have thought my father's will was relevant, Inspector. It isn't as if he was a rich man. As it happens, I am his only child and he made me sole beneficiary.'

'So what will you inherit, Mrs Elsworth?'

'Well, I hadn't thought about it. I know he has between two and three thousand in the bank plus this house and what bit of furniture there is, that's all.'

'Is the mortgage paid off?'

'Yes, I'm glad to say that it is. He paid that off years ago.'

Angel nodded thoughtfully. 'Good. Good.'

He wished his mortgage was paid off. He wondered how her flower business was doing. If the rent wasn't too high and sales were healthy, she could be doing very nicely, even in the recession.

'Do you have an accountant, Mrs Elsworth?'

'Of course. King and Company on Victoria Road. Only a small practice … I can afford his charges. Why?'

'Might need to speak to him,' he said.

She flushed round the neck and the redness spread to her cheeks.

'It would be in absolute confidence,' he said. 'I want to eliminate you from our suspect list just as much as you do. In cases of murder the family is always suspected first and needs to be eliminated.'

She turned away, pulled a tissue out of her overall pocket and dabbed her eyes. 'It's outrageous … what you are insinuating.'

'I'm sorry, Mrs Elsworth. Murder is a rotten business. But don't you worry. If you are innocent, you have nothing to worry about.'

He waited a few moments for her to recover her composure, then said, 'Your daughter, Moira. I need to speak to her.'

'Moira knows nothing. She can't help you. What do you want to see her for?'

'To exclude her from our investigations. If she's innocent she's nothing to worry about either.'

'Oh dear. Isn't it enough that we've lost a father and a grandfather without being accused of being responsible for his murder?'

'I'm not accusing anybody of anything. Just tell me how I can get in touch with her. Where does she work?'

'She's between jobs at the moment. I can probably reach her on her mobile,' she said. She took out a phone from the pocket in her overall, tapped several buttons and put it to her ear. Then she looked at Angel sternly and said, 'Whatever arrangement you make to interview her, I want to be present, Inspector.'

Angel shook his head slowly. 'She's over eighteen, isn't she?'

Christine Elsworth looked away from him and began to speak into the phone. 'It's me, darling. Listen. I am with that policeman I told you about … yes, that's the one. Now he wants to meet you … to interview you … to ask you some questions. … I don't know. … He's at the shop…. You can? Well, where are you now? … Hold on, I'll ask him.'

She held the phone away from her mouth and said, 'She's the other side of town, Inspector. She was going to drop in here to see me this morning anyway. She can be here in five or ten minutes if that would be convenient to you.'

Angel nodded. 'That would be fine.'

She returned to the phone. 'Marvellous, darling … look forward to seeing you … well, bring him with you … he can wait in the shop … well, that's up to him, isn't it … 'bye.'

She closed the phone and dropped it into her overall pocket. 'She's shopping with her new boyfriend.'

Angel looked at her. It sounded interesting. 'What's he like, the new boyfriend?'

'Oh, very smart. Nicely spoken. Clean. Usually wears a suit. Much more civilized than the unshaven, tattooed, scruffy, jean-clad layabouts I've seen her with of late. She might bring him with her. I hope you won't say anything that might affect their relationship, Inspector. My mother made life difficult and embarrassing for me and my acquaintances when I was young. I vowed I would not be so critical of Moira's friends.'

Angel shrugged. 'Have you any thoughts on who might have wanted to murder your father?'

'No. None at all.'

'Nobody, as far as you know, had a grudge or a disagreement with your father … anything at all?'

'No. He never spoke of anything. And we were very close, particularly lately.'

'And his granddaughter, your daughter, Moira, did he get on well with her?'

She glared at Angel. 'Of *course* he did,' she said. 'What do you think we are, a family of heathens?'

Angel was surprised by her response. 'A simple "yes" would have been a more than adequate reply, Mrs Elsworth. Now, about Nancy Quinn. What can you tell me about her?'

'Do you think she murdered my father?'

'We are leaving that question open for the time being. Did Nancy Quinn come with good references?'

'Well Inspector, I can't say that she did. That's not to say that she came with bad references. I was so desperate I believe I took her at face value. At the interview, I thought she was satisfactory and as there was nothing valuable in the house, I didn't think I needed to bother about her honesty. I just needed her to see that Dad was clean, comfortable and well fed. I never thought of anything else.'

'So you knew nothing of her history or her background?'

'I knew she had no formal qualifications. She admitted that straightaway….'

Angel heard the girl in the shop say, 'Good morning, Moira,' behind him.

It was followed by a rustle of clothes.

Moira Elsworth entered the little workroom.

Christine Elsworth slid off the stool and stepped up to her daughter, arms outstretched.

'Darling,' Christine said and turned her cheek towards Moira, who pressed her lips briefly on it.

'How lovely to see you,' Christine said.

Moira looked uncertain and said, 'Yes, hello, Mummy.'

Angel looked the girl up and down.

Moira was a 20-year-old stunner in a summer dress.

She turned to Angel, smiled and said, 'And this is the famous policeman you were telling me about? How do you do, Inspector?'

He smiled and nodded. She was easy to smile at.

'I've read about you in the papers,' Moira Elsworth said. 'It said that – like the Mounties – you always get your man. I've got to ask you, is that really true?'

Angel licked his bottom lip. He hated that tag. Because inevitably the odds were that a case would crop up where there simply wasn't enough evidence and he would not be able to prove the guilt of a suspect. He hoped it wouldn't happen in this case. He swallowed, then said, 'It has been up to now, miss.'

'The Inspector wants to ask you a few questions, Moira,' Christine Elsworth said.

'Call me Moira, Inspector please. And let's hope you get your man this time.'

'Let's hope so, Moira,' he said. 'Let's hope so. And thank you. But I need your help. And your mother's right: I do want to ask you a few questions.'

'Excuse me, Inspector,' Christine Elsworth said. She looked at Moira and said, 'Did Charles bring you – is he in the shop waiting for you?'

Angel saw the muscles round Moira's mouth tighten. 'No, Mummy,' Moira said. 'He dropped me off and went off to fill up with petrol.'

Angel looked at Christine. He wasn't pleased.

'Sorry,' Christine Elsworth said. 'I didn't want him hanging around, that's all....'

'Moira,' Angel said. 'Did you get on well with your grandfather?'

'Oh yes, Inspector. He was a lovely man ... a substitute father to me for years until his memory went about two years ago. Then he didn't seem to respond much to us any more. He would look at me and smile. He knew I was a friendly face, but he didn't seem to know who I was exactly.'

'Did you see much of him lately?'

'Not as much as I should have done, I know,' Moira said. 'I called in to see him about a week ago, briefly. He seemed fine. He was watching a cowboy film on the television. He turned it off when we came in. I said there was no need. He didn't know me and, of course, he didn't know Charles, but he *was* pleased to see us. He started on with his rambling, so I asked him if there was anything he wanted. He didn't seem to understand. He looked warm and comfortable, and tolerably happy. We couldn't understand what he was on about and he didn't listen to us, or wouldn't listen, so, after a while, we left.'

Angel frowned. 'And what was he rambling on about?' he said.

Christine Elsworth butted in and said, 'Just words that don't make sense repeated and repeated.'

Angel looked hard at her, then turned back to Moira Elsworth and said, 'What exactly did he say? Can you remember any of it?'

Christine Elsworth said, 'I've told you. It's just words that don't make any sense repeated over and over again.'

Angel glared at her. He was furious. 'Mrs Elsworth, if you can't keep quiet and let your daughter answer for herself, I'll book you for obstructing the police in the execution of their duty.'

Moira said, 'As far as I could make out, he was saying, "There're thousands and thousands." He kept repeating that, then, sometimes he said, "There're thousands and thousands of pounds." That's all. He was trying to tell us something, but I don't know what.'

Angel rubbed his chin.

'Tell me, Moira. Where were you on Sunday night at around ten o'clock?'

'Ten o'clock? I was with Charles at his flat in Tunistone.'

'If I'm allowed to speak,' Christine said, looking at Angel, 'I can confirm that that is so. I spoke to her on the phone about then ... only to find out what sort of a day she'd had. She said that she was tired, having been out all day with Charles in Knaresborough. Mother Shipton's Cave and all that.'

'Oh yes,' Moira said. 'We rowed up and down the river ... I was tired out. Got in about eight o'clock.'

'I was at home finishing the ironing,' Christine Elsworth said.

'Thank you very much, both of you,' Angel said. 'I think that's about it for now.'

They both looked pleased.

He turned towards the way out, then he looked back.

'One more thing, Moira,' he said. 'Will you call into the station some time soon, and bring your friend, Charles ... erm, what's his name?' Then he paused and looked at her with eyebrows raised.

'Morris,' Moira said. 'His name is Charles Morris.'

'Morris, thank you. Yes, Charles Morris. We need your finger-prints – *and* his – to eliminate them from those found in your grandfather's house. All right?'

'All right, Inspector,' Moira said, sounding confident, but then she half closed her eyes and licked her bottom lip as her stomach turned over and a shiver went down her spine.

Angel left Christine and Moira Elsworth at the flower kiosk and returned to the BMW parked down High Street. He got inside, pulled out his mobile and tapped in a number.

Ahmed answered. 'Yes, sir?'

'Ah yes, lad. Find out what you can about a Charles Morris. There's not much I can tell you. I expect he'll be in the age range twenty-five to forty-five. See if he's known to us, and ring me back. And is Ted Scrivens there?'

'Yes, sir. He's at his desk.'

'Let me speak to him, will you?'

'Yes sir, just a minute.'

'DC Scrivens here, sir.'

'Ted, I want you to go to Nancy Quinn's flat and look for a newspaper dated last Sunday. It should still be there. It might have been binned, but wherever it is, find it and stuff it in an evidence bag. Also find a bottle of milk, probably in the fridge; it might be a plastic bottle, put that in a bag also. Take both items to Don Taylor to see if there are any good prints on either of them.'

'Right, sir.'

'Hang on. I want you to do something else. DS Crisp has found a witness who saw a man entering Nancy Quinn's flat at around ten o'clock on Sunday morning last with those two items. Find the nearest, likely place a man might go at ten o'clock on a cold, May Sunday morning to buy a bottle of milk and a newspaper, if he was bunked up with Nancy Quinn. It's not likely to be far from there. And I can't be certain, but I would expect him to get both items from the same shop. I want a full description of the man. He could possibly be her murderer. See what you can do. All right?'

'Right, sir.'

Angel closed the mobile. His heart felt lighter. He was quite pleased he had given that highly critical job to Scrivens. There was a young detective who was not academically gifted, but he was very hard-working, reliable and honest.

He pocketed the mobile and started the car engine.

It was only a couple of side streets away to Victoria Road. He drove the car slowly so that he could read the painted windows and, in some cases, the brass plates of the many solicitors, account-ants, estate agents, veterinary surgeries, dentists and sandwich shops all crammed together in that short road. He saw a plate that read: *King and Co., Accountants*. That was the one he wanted.

He stopped the BMW and made his way up to the door. The card in the glass panel in the door read *Enter*. He turned the door-knob and went in.

The top corner of the door hit a lever that caused a large curly spring with a bell in the centre to bounce about, making a loud ring. A man wearing spectacles with thick lenses and spidery frames came through a door into the hall. He was dressed in a shiny blue suit, collar and tie.

Angel introduced himself and asked to see the person who dealt with the business affairs of Mrs Christine Elsworth.

'That would be me, Inspector. Andrew King. There is only me. Please come through.'

Angel followed him into an office comprising a big desk, six long tables and three chairs. The desk, chairs, tables and part of the floor were covered with piles of papers, letters, brown envelopes, account books, ledgers and tax tables.

'Sit down,' King said, pointing to a chair; then he saw the clutter of papers on it.

'Sorry,' he said. He rushed over, gathered everything up until he had an arm-load and then looked around for somewhere to put it. He decided that the floor was the only option. He eventually selected a space and deposited it all there.

'There we are,' he said. 'Sorry about all this. The year-end. It's my busiest time.'

'Thank you,' Angel said.

King settled down at his desk, leaned forward and said, 'Now, Inspector, what do you want to know?'

'How long have you known Christine Elsworth?'

'A few years. I can't remember exactly how many. Fourteen or fifteen.'

'So you know all about her financial situation?'

'I suppose I do, but that would be confidential, Inspector, without specific instructions from her.'

'All I want is a general picture, Mr King. I could get a warrant to have her affairs looked into, if I had to, and HMRC will always cooperate with us if need be and tell us all that their records showed, so there's no need to be so guarded. All I need to know is how wealthy she is, how successful her flower business is and whether or not she has any money troubles.'

'Well, erm, she's pretty well off, Inspector. She paid off the mortgage on her house years ago. The flower business is flourishing, despite the recession. The profit on flowers can be as much as 300 per cent, you know. Her turnover goes up each year and so does her profit. The fixed lease on the shop has a few years left to run, so I don't see why she shouldn't continue to make a healthy profit each year over the next few years at least.'

Angel pursed his lips. 'Right. Did you know her father?'

'I met him some years ago. Nice old gentleman. Lived to a ripe old age. I was sorry to read that he had died a few days ago, didn't he?'

'I'm sad to say that he was murdered.'

King's eyes and mouth opened wide. 'Really? Oh dear. I am so sorry to hear that. How is Christine? I must phone her. Oh dear.'

'She's managing, I think, under the circumstances,' he said.

Angel thanked King and left the office. He looked at his watch. It was 1.45. He decided he'd better return to the station and see what had come in.

EIGHT

Angel had only just arrived in his office when there was a knock at the door.

'Come in,' Angel said.

It was Ahmed.

'You asked me to look up Charles Morris on the PNC, sir. Well, I've done that.'

'Aye, and what did you find?'

'There were eight of that name, sir. You said an age range of twenty-five to forty-five. Well, sir, there were only two in that age range, but one is dead and the other is in Maidstone prison for armed robbery. He's midway through a stretch of fifteen years. So I phoned Maidstone and spoke to the head officer. He said that he could confirm that *their* Charles Morris was definitely locked up in a cell last Sunday night and not on probation or early release or anything like that.'

Angel thought it was remarkable that, unprompted, Ahmed had had the initiative to follow the inquiry through to Maidstone and get all that information. He rubbed his chin.

'Well done, lad,' he said. 'That means that the PNC has no record of the Charles Morris who is a close friend of Moira Elsworth.'

'That's right, sir.'

Angel rubbed his chin harder. He needed to know more about him.

'Ahmed, Morris lives in Tunistone. Phone round the doctor's surgeries in the area. There can't be more than a couple. Find out which practice he is with. Then ask them for his National Insurance number, and carefully write it down. That's the key that will allow us to find out his health history, his age, addresses, his past and present earnings and tax position, and more than he knows himself.'

'Right, sir. I didn't know he was a suspect.'

'He may be perfectly kosher. We have to get at the facts. That's what we're doing, lad, collecting the facts.'

'Phew. Right, sir,' Ahmed said. 'I'll see what I can do.'

'Well done, Ahmed. Go to it.'

Ahmed went out.

Angel rubbed his chin. He thought that there was something odd about an old man being pushed down the stairs, possibly by his carer, possibly by somebody else, then his carer being brutally attacked and stabbed many times. The murderer of the young woman carer was clearly off his rocker, in which case he might very well do it again, especially if a woman – particularly an attractive woman – was in his way.

Ever since Taylor had told him about the message daubed by the killer of Nancy Quinn on the bedroom wall and showed him the photograph of it, he had been eager to see the provocative message for himself.

He pushed the swivel chair away from the desk, stood up and made his way out of the office to the door. He would leave quickly before anybody delayed him with any more unhelpful information.

As he made his way up the corridor, he saw DS Flora Carter coming down, making a beeline for him. When they were two metres apart, she said, 'Sir.'

Angel waved his hand. 'Can't stop now, Flora,' he said without slackening his pace. 'Report on Nancy Quinn?'

'Yes, sir.'

'Come with me. I'm going to her place now.'

Flora turned round and walked at his side.

'You can give me your report in the car on the way,' he said.

They got into the BMW and when he had turned safely out of the police car park, Angel said, 'Right, Flora, what've you got?'

Flora Carter, referring to her notebook, said, 'Nancy Quinn, sir. I found nothing of particular interest. She was born in 1988. She lived with her parents on Canal Street, Bromersley. They're both dead now. Father died in 2000 and her mother 2006.'

'Anything odd about their deaths? What did they die of?'

'Natural causes. Father died of a heart attack and her mother of breast cancer. Nancy went to Cemetery Road School. Left when she was sixteen and went straight to nurses' college on Blair Avenue, but didn't finish the course.'

'Blair Avenue? Where's that?'

'It used to be called Thatcher Avenue.'

Angel blinked, then smiled.

Flora continued: 'The principal there said that Nancy couldn't afford to continue the course even though she was subsidized by the council. The principal said that she discovered afterwards that Nancy was interested in a particular young man. Anyway, she left the college at eighteen and worked for two years at the Eventide Home for the Elderly on Sheffield Road, as a trainee carer. The manageress there said she left in August 2008, when she was twenty. She told me Nancy said the money wasn't good enough for her. The manageress mentioned that she often did her best to stop good staff from leaving, that it was always cheaper than teaching a new girl from scratch. However, in this case, she said, she was happy to let her go.'

'In other words she was no good?'

'That's the implication, sir.'

Angel had to apply the brake to the car because of a traffic light. He turned to Flora and said, 'You didn't get the name of the young man, did you?'

'No, sir. The principal simply said that she had frequently seen a young man waiting for her at the end of the lectures. He used to ride off with her on the back of his very noisy motorbike.'

'Did she know what he looked like?'

'She said she wouldn't be able to describe him now, but she seems to recall that he was a pleasant, clean, presentable young man.'

'Hmmm. And where did Nancy go after she left the Eventide Home?'

'That's where the trail ran out, sir. I couldn't pick it up anywhere. Work and Pensions said that according to their records, she wasn't in any employment, and was receiving state benefit.'

'Did Work and Pensions tell you that if she was receiving cash in hand for work, without declaring it, which is illegal of course, it wouldn't show up on their records?'

Flora smiled. 'Well, I don't expect she declared her earnings from Christine Elsworth.'

The light changed to green so Angel put the car in gear and let in the clutch. He turned left onto Jubilee Park Road. He hadn't far to travel along there to Commodore House.

'It's a pity you couldn't get info on the man Nancy was going out with. Did any of the other people there know anything at all about her young man?'

'Most of the staff weren't even there between 2006 and 2008, sir. Staff doing those sorts of jobs don't stay long.'

He nodded. He knew she was right. 'Anything else?'

'No, sir. Sorry.'

'It all fits the style of girl she was. Struggling on her own, without parents to guide her and lean on.'

He knocked down the indicator stalk on the steering wheel, and turned right onto the concrete forecourt of Commodore House.

They got out of the car and took the lift up to Nancy Quinn's flat.

There was a uniformed policeman still outside the door of number 21.

'Good afternoon, sir,' the constable said, throwing up a salute.

'Good afternoon, lad,' Angel said. 'Are the SOC people still in there?'

'Yes, sir. DS Taylor has just come back and there are one or two others in there.'

Angel nodded, pressed down the door handle and walked into the little flat.

Taylor was speaking to one of his team. When he saw them he broke off and came across. 'Good afternoon, sir.'

'Found anything of interest, Don?' Angel said.

'Well, sir. I believe we have eight different specimens of hair – not hers – vacuumed off her clothes, sir. But there is no telling whether they are relevant or not.'

'No, but let's be optimistic. By the way, I sent young Scrivens over to try to retrieve a particular newspaper and a bottle of milk....'

'It's in hand, sir. He gave me your message. But there was no trace of the paper. We looked in the bins and absolutely everywhere. But we think we've got the right bottle of milk. In fact it was the only one. It does have fingerprints on it and identification is being sought at the station, as we speak.'

'Good. Apart from the hair specimens, are there any other traces? Prints or anything?'

'We've not found any clear, recent fingerprints. The obvious places where we would expect to find prints have been deliberately wiped clean with something woollen such as a glove. Also all the cutlery, for example, and some of the pots, both dirty and clean, have been wiped over.'

Angel pursed his lips.

'Unusual,' Flora Carter said.

'Yes, Flora,' Angel said, 'which makes me think our murderer is a psycho. They can be very devious and have an amazingly clear discernment of a character's probable reactions.'

Taylor shook his head when he heard what Angel had said. He didn't like it one bit. 'You really think it's a psycho, sir?' he said. 'I remember before when we had a psycho. It took three of us to hold him down to handcuff him. And he almost wrecked your office.'

Flora Carter looked uncomfortable.

'Yes. He was a big, athletic chap. Tore the tongue out of one of his victims, and tried to nick a man's lifetime collection of highly valuable snuffboxes. He's safely locked up now, Flora. He's in Wilefowle High Security Hospital. Murderers come in assorted guises. We can't pick and choose. Now, how is tracing the calls on her mobile coming along?'

'It's being attended to, sir … at the station.'

'Good. Let me know as soon as you can.'

'Of course, sir.'

'Any prohibited substances, weapons, pornography, cash, drugs or gold?'

'No, sir. If there had been anything of value here – and I don't think there would have been much – I reckon the assailant would have gone through the place methodically, drawer by drawer, cupboard by cupboard, and taken away every note and coin, and piece of jewellery in the place or on her person. The purse in her handbag had credit cards in it, but no cash. And I noticed that the body had no watch, rings or earrings on it.'

Angel said: 'Aye. Fits the psycho pattern absolutely. Thoroughness and attention to detail.'

Taylor nodded.

'Mac said that the murder weapon was a short knife with a serrated blade, possibly a steak knife. Have you come across it?'

He shook his head. 'If it had been there, we would have seen it.'

'He must have taken it with him.'

'In my report you will see that the bathroom sink has signs of watered-down blood where he probably washed himself and/or that knife, and a blue towel found on a towel rail, which he also used.'

Angel nodded, then he looked around the room and said, 'Which room has that message daubed on a wall?'

'The bedroom, sir. Through that door,' Taylor said, indicating the door they were facing.

Angel took a deep breath through his teeth and marched into the room. Flora Carter followed close behind.

The room contained a typical three-piece bedroom suite in pinewood, an odd chair and an odd bedside cabinet, all painted pink. Nancy Quinn's mountain of clothes had all been cleared away. There were bottles, jars and other containers of all kinds of make-up, hair and beauty products crammed onto the dressing table and the bedside cabinet. Everything was covered in aluminium powder where the fingerprint expert had been looking for that giveaway print. The walls had been papered with a plain paper which presumably over the years had been distempered several times. The wall facing the bed had the message daubed in bloody capital letters about eighteen to twenty centimetres high: Inspector A – don't get in my way.

The muscles round Angel's mouth tightened as he stared in silence at the grotesque words.

Flora Carter looked at his face. After a few moments she said, 'What are you thinking, sir?'

He turned up his nose and said, 'I'll get in his way all right. And I hope to get there before he murders anybody else.'

*

It was 5.30 when Angel arrived home. He was weary.

As he drove the BMW into the garage, he thought that he seemed to have rushed around without achieving very much. He ran through his doings … he had seen the bloody message from the murderer, warning him not to get in the way … Don Taylor had told him that there was a fresh set of prints on the back of old Mr Piddington's wheelchair that might be those of the murderer… and a man had been seen entering Nancy Quinn's flat with a paper and bottle of milk on the same day as she was brutally murdered, someone who might have left his prints on the bottle … and he had seen Andrew King, accountant to Christine Elsworth, who had told him that his client's finances were healthy. A lot to think about, but none of it helped him find the murderer.

He reached the back door and put the key in the lock.

Mary met him at the door. She put her arms round him and kissed him on the lips. He squeezed her and kissed her back.

It was unusual to get such a greeting from her after sixteen years of marriage.

He held her tight and pushed her away to enable him to take a good look into her eyes. He frowned and said, 'What's the matter, love?'

'I thought you might be put out … maybe upset,' she said, smiling and patting him gently on the cheek.

Angel frowned. 'What about?'

'About what the Chief Constable said.'

He had almost forgotten that he had had an appointment that morning with the big boss. He forced a grin. 'What do *you* know about what he said?'

'I don't know anything about it. But it's been on mind all day. Tell me … what was it about?'

Angel turned round, closed the door and remembered what the superintendent had said about gangs, and he'd given the case of the bank robbers and what had happened to the bank manager's wife. Angel had no intention of telling Mary about that. There were times such as when a policeman was killed in the line of duty that Mary took it to heart, got very upset and said that she wished he was out of the force and in a safe job such as working in the HMRC office.

'Actually we didn't see the Chief,' he said. 'He was at the big golf tournament.'

Her mouth dropped open.

'In Scotland,' he added.

'Golf tournament … in Scotland?'

He passed her, went to the fridge, took out a can of German beer, found a glass in the cupboard next to it, and poured some out. He took a sip. Then he looked back at her.

'Well, *what* happened then?' she said. 'What was it about?'

'Oh, well, he briefed Harker. And he had Haydn Asquith and me in his office. It was about gangs. Particularly gangs robbing banks. It wasn't that interesting.'

Her eyebrows knitted together. 'Is that all?'

'Yes,' he lied. 'What's for tea?' he said quickly. 'I must go up and take this suit off. I don't want to get it creased.'

He drank more of the beer, emptied the remaining contents of the can into his glass, then took another swig.

Mary glared at him. 'What are you hiding? All these quick, diversionary tactics, Michael Angel. I know you of old. What did he really say?'

'I've told you,' he said. Then he added: 'And you're the one doing the diversionary tactics. I said, what's for tea?'

'Ham salad, strawberries and ice cream,' she snapped, continuing to eye him closely.

'Very nice,' he said, quickly turning towards the hall. 'I'm going upstairs. Get out of this suit … keep it nice and pressed. Won't be a jiffy.'

NINE

It was 8.28 a.m. the following morning when Angel arrived at his office. He glared at the pile of post, circulars, letters and reports on his desk, then picked up the phone and tapped in a number.

'Is DS Crisp anywhere on the horizon, lad?' he said into the mouthpiece.

'He's at his desk, sir,' Ahmed said.

'Huh. Right, lad,' he said. 'Tell him I want him.' He banged the phone down into the cradle.

There was a knock at the door and Crisp came in.

Angel looked up at him.

Crisp felt very guilty. 'I was just coming anyway, sir,' he said.

Angel doubted it. 'I asked you to phone me on my mobile as soon as you had the information from the witness. It's very urgent, lad.'

'I didn't get to see him until late yesterday afternoon. I would have had to ring you at home. I didn't think you'd want bothering.'

'This is a murder case, lad. I always want bothering. You've rung me at home many times before.'

Crisp looked at him with an expression of surprised innocence.

Angel shook his head, knowing it was hopeless reasoning with him and said, 'You'd better have a good description of that chap.'

Crisp turned over a few pages of his notebook. 'I have, sir. Ray Rich said that the man he saw was about six feet tall, dark hair, probably in his early thirties and had a cherubic face—'

'Cherubic face? What's that mean?'

'Face like a cherub, sir.'

'And what's a cherub look like?'

Crisp shrugged slightly, looked aimlessly around the office, then looked back at Angel and said, 'Dunno exactly. That's what the witness said. I suppose he meant young looking, chubby cheeks, a bit like those angels on Christmas cards.'

Angel was impressed at his totally sensible explanation. Then he suddenly remembered that somebody else had described the man he was looking for as cherubic. It was Mrs Roman, the lady who lived next door to Nancy Quinn.

Angel pursed his lips. Was it really possible that he had two independent witnesses using the same word to describe the man who may very well turn out to be the murderer of their neighbour? This was progress. Progress indeed.

'What else?' Angel said. 'Was he clean-shaven?'

'Oh yes, sir.'

'Great. What else?'

'Ray Rich said that he thought he was wearing a stone-coloured raincoat.'

'Stone-coloured?

'Yes, sir, and he was carrying the *Sunday Telegraph* and a plastic bottle of milk.'

'*Sunday Telegraph*. That's even better. Did he speak with an accent?'

'He didn't speak. Neither of them spoke.'

'Did he smell of anything? I don't only mean body odour. I mean mints or cigars or garlic or Vicks or soap or anything at all.'

'No, sir. I went through all that.'

'Right, lad. And you've nothing else to add?'

Crisp frowned, then said, 'No, sir.'

Angel rubbed his chin, then said, 'Sounds like we've got a psycho for a murderer, who is well turned out, attracts women, speaks nicely, likes Beethoven and is kind to animals.'

'Have you anybody in mind, sir?'

'Yes, lad. About half the population of the UK.'

There was a knock on the door.

'Come in,' Angel called. It was Ahmed.

'What is it, lad?'

'I've got Charles Morris's National Insurance number, sir,' Ahmed said.

Angel smiled. 'Ah. You found his doctor, then?'

'Yes, sir. Morris had some pain in an ear in December last, sir, so he had to register with a GP's practice to get treated.'

'Great stuff. What was up with him?'

'Don't know, sir. Didn't sound serious. He had his ears syringed and he's not been back.'

'Good lad,' he said to Ahmed. 'Give the number to DS Crisp here.'

'Right, sir.'

Angel then turned to Crisp and said, 'Find out all you can about Charles Morris. He's recently started taking an interest in Ernest Piddington's granddaughter, Moira Elsworth. She's a bit of an eye-knocker, but he's at least twenty years older than she is.'

Crisp's eyebrows went up. 'Right, sir,' he said, grinning. He turned and made for the door.

Angel noticed the grin. 'And she's too young and innocent for you, Crisp,' he called. 'So don't get any fanciful ideas.'

Crisp smiled. 'If she's over seventeen, sir, she's not too young.'

'It's Charles Morris I want you to look into, not Moira Elsworth.'

'Yes, sir,' he said.

Both Crisp and Ahmed went out.

Angel watched the door close and shook his head.

He glanced at the pile of post, envelopes and reports directly in front of him. It looked bigger and bigger. He leaned back in the chair. He tried to clear his mind so that he could consider what he might have neglected to do to progress the inquiry, and then, what he ought to do next. He was still cogitating when there was a knock at the door.

'Come in,' he called.

It was Don Taylor. He was carrying two big brown envelopes with the word EVIDENCE printed across each of them in red ink. 'Have you a minute, sir?'

'Yes. Sit down,' Angel said.

'We've finished at both Ernest Piddington's house and at Nancy Quinn's. And there were no illegal or suspicious items in either house. We have eight hair samples taken off the woman's clothes. These have been sent to Wetherby to have their DNA checked. The prints on the bottle of milk from Nancy Quinn's fridge are hers and there are no others.'

'That's a disappointment Don, but it confirms that she was alive at ten o'clock on Sunday morning. Anything else?'

'I regret to say that we have still not found the owner of the prints on the back of Piddington's wheelchair.'

Angel's face muscles tightened as he rubbed his chin. 'We'll have to keep our eyes on that.'

Taylor then put the EVIDENCE envelopes on the desk in front of Angel and said, 'And these are the personal effects of Nancy Quinn and Ernest Piddington, sir. That's about it.'

'I'm still awaiting the history of the phone calls on Nancy Quinn's mobile, Don.'

'We're working on it, sir, but we are rather overwhelmed with everything happening at once.'

'Let Ahmed do it. He's done it before. Would that help?'

'Oh yes, sir. I'll pass that on to him. And I'll let you have my written report on both cases ASAP.'

'Right, lad.'

Taylor went out and closed the door.

Angel was disappointed that so much promising evidence was turning out to be useless. However, it was quite usual, and he had always found that as well as hard work, you needed a bit of good luck to solve any mystery or crime.

In considering the murder of Ernest Piddington, he had not entirely eliminated Christine Elsworth, his daughter, as a suspect. She had motive, opportunity and means. She inherited everything. On the other hand, she didn't seem to have inherited very much. Also, she had shown every sign – apparently genuinely – of being a loving, caring daughter. Then there was Moira Elsworth. But she had no motive that he was aware of. Also he was looking closely at Charles Morris, her boyfriend. Then there was Nancy Quinn. She didn't have a motive as far as Angel could see, but she did have opportunity and the means. However, if she had murdered the old man she'd be out of a job. There didn't seem to be any other suspects at that time.

The murderer of Nancy Quinn was certainly a man. But who would have the impudence to write up on a wall, in the victim's blood, *Inspector A – keep out of my way*? The message suggested that the murderer actually *knew* Angel, and that he had had a close personal encounter with him in his work as a police officer, a witness, or offender or member of Neighbourhood Watch or in his private life. Perhaps the man was a neighbour, someone Angel had met in the pub, or an acquaintance he might have met briefly in the park, in a shop or on holiday.

He sighed and gently poured the contents of one of the EVIDENCE envelopes onto his desk top.

It contained a small handbag, not much bigger than a purse. He opened it and found a credit card, a handkerchief, a lipstick, a small compact, a ballpoint pen and a part tube of mints. That was all.

Angel frowned, rubbed his chin, then put the items back in the handbag and the handbag back into the envelope. He reached out for the phone and tapped in a single digit to SOCO's office.

Taylor answered.

'Is everything here from Nancy Quinn's purse, Don?' Angel said.

'Yes, sir,' Taylor said. 'There wasn't any money. I thought I had mentioned that.'

'It's not that, Don. It's something very strange. I didn't find any keys. There should be at least one key there, the key to her flat.'

'There were no keys in the purse, sir. And, in fact, we didn't find any keys inside the flat either.'

Angel frowned. 'Right, lad. Thank you.'

He ended the call and dropped the phone into its cradle.

He sighed and gently poured the contents of the second EVIDENCE envelope onto his desk top.

It included an old, battered leather wallet containing no money, and two bank credit cards with expiry dates 06 1986 and 02 1989. An old age pensioner's card to allow treble points if you shopped at Cheapo's supermarket on Wednesdays. In the big opening at the back of the wallet was folded the paper-style driving licence. He pulled it out and opened it up. It showed that it was a clean licence and valid up to 1989. There seemed to be nothing there of interest. Angel opened up the pocket to push the stiff paper licence back down when he felt something in the way. He peered inside. It was light brown, the same colour as the wallet itself. Curious, he fished it out with a paperknife. At first it looked like a piece of the lining of the wallet, but it wasn't, it was a small newspaper cutting scrunched up and brown with age. He carefully opened it and straightened it out. The tiny black printing in bold letters read: *Bottomley, Ronald Arthur*. Then in ordinary print he read, "*12 December 1926 – 16 May 1986. Beloved husband of Bettina Aimee, father of Sean and Patrice. Service 10 a.m. Wednesday next, St Cecilia's Church, followed by interment at Tunistone Road cemetery.*

He squeezed the lobe of an ear between finger and thumb, and read the cutting again. Then he pulled an old envelope from his inside pocket which was covered with his small writing. He peered at it carefully and eventually found what he was looking for. He reached out for the phone and tapped in a number. When he heard the ringing-out tone he eased back in the chair.

It was eventually answered. 'Christine's flower shop,' she said.

'Michael Angel here, Mrs Elsworth, good morning to you. Just a couple of points. Did Nancy Quinn happen to have a key to your father's house?'

'Yes, Inspector, she did. Why?'

'Oh, just curious, that's all. We have not been able to find one among her things. Also I am in the process of going through your father's possessions and I have come across the announcement of a man's death, Ronald Arthur Bottomley ... it goes back to 1986. Do you know who the man was and what connection he had with your father?'

'No, I'm sorry, Inspector. I have no idea. I have never heard the name.'

'All right, thank you, Mrs Elsworth. It was just a long shot. I thought you might have been able to help us. If it comes to you, please let me know. Thank you very much, goodbye.'

He ended the call and replaced the phone.

He wasn't really happy with her answer. She didn't query the name. She didn't even ask him to repeat it, and her answer came out too quickly for her to have given it any careful thought. There was definitely something fishy about Christine Elsworth.

Now he had another couple of puzzles to solve. Where were Nancy Quinn's keys, and who the heck was Ronald Arthur Bottomley?

If the man was alive today, he'd be eighty-seven, five years younger than Ernest Piddington. He was buried at St Cecilia's. That meant he must have been a Roman Catholic. So what? That wouldn't help much to identify the man. What part did he play in Ernest Piddington's life that made him bother to cut the announcement out and save it all those years?

There was a knock at the door. It was Scrivens. His eyes were glowing. 'Can I have a word, sir?' he said brightly.

Angel noticed the enthusiasm. It sounded promising.

'Come in, lad. Sit down. I take it you've found our man?'

'I think so, sir. There's a little newsagent's round the corner from the Commodore flats. On the corner of Commodore Street and Peel Avenue. He does more trade on a Sunday morning than he does the rest of the week. He remembers a tall man, about forty, coming in for a bottle of milk and a paper.'

Angel's heart began to thump through his shirt. 'Was he able to describe him?' he said.

'Only in broad terms, sir,' Scrivens said, taking out his notebook and finding the page. 'He said he looked about forty, tall, black hair, good tan, looked well to do, wearing a smart raincoat. When I pressed him about the colour of the raincoat he said that he thought it was a light shade, fawn or stone-coloured.'

Something in Angel's stomach did a fandango. 'That's our man.'

'He's certain he bought the *Sunday Telegraph*,' Scrivens said, 'because he doesn't sell too many of them round there. He only orders five copies and he knows pretty well who buys them. Also the man offered him a £50 note which he doesn't accept any more because he was caught with a counterfeit one once. When he refused it, the man wasn't pleased, but he eventually paid him with a £20 note. He's not sure of the time. He's so busy, he doesn't know about time. He's in the shop by 5.15 and he closes about one o'clock because he's pretty well sold out of his papers by then.'

'That's great, lad. It fits in exactly with the description we already have. He is almost certainly the man who murdered Nancy Quinn.'

Scrivens beamed when he saw how elated the boss was.

Angel rubbed his chin. 'Now I've got another little job for you, lad.'

Scrivens took out his notebook, opened it up and looked across the desk.

'I want you to find out about a man called Ronald Arthur Bottomley.'

TEN

It was 8.28 a.m. Thursday morning, 9 May.

Angel had arrived at the station and was making his way down the corridor. As he reached the CID office, he stopped and looked in. Several officers were busy at their desks and Ahmed nearest the door was staring at a computer screen. Sensing that he was being watched, Ahmed raised his eyes from the screen. Seeing Angel, he stood up and said, 'Oh. Good morning, sir. Looking for me?'

'DS Carter,' Angel said.

Ahmed glanced round. 'She's not here, sir. Do you want me to find her?'

'Thanks, lad. Ask her to come to my office ASAP. Are you still checking Nancy Quinn's mobile phone calls?'

'Yes, sir,' Ahmed said, looking surprised. 'DS Taylor told me—'

'That's all right, lad. As soon as you've done, let me know.'

'Right, sir. I've only about six numbers left to check.'

Angel nodded and made for his own office.

It was only a few moments later that there was a knock on the door. It was DS Carter.

'Good morning, sir, you wanted me?'

'Come in, Flora. Sit down,' he said, rubbing his chin. 'Do you know ... last night I was thinking about Christine Elsworth and that little flower kiosk of hers. It's so tiny. Her accountant says she does very well. I just wondered *how* well. It wasn't very busy when I was there, and she wasn't exactly crammed out with stock either.'

'Well, sir, with cut flowers, I don't suppose you want more stock than you can expect to sell pretty quickly.'

'True. When I was there, she only had a dozen or so large vases with ten or twenty flowers in each vase. What's a single flower worth to buy on average, do you think? 50p?'

'Depends. Maybe a bit less. Say 40p.'

'Right, 40p. That roughs up to ... 200 flowers at 40p each ... that's about ... eighty pounds. She wouldn't have made a fortune if she had sold every bloom in the shop that day, would she? She's got staff wages, rent, rates, light, heat, phone, delivery vehicle, petrol, depreciation, insurance, security, bank charges, advertising, wrapping boxes and paper and cards and—'

The phone rang. Angel glared at it. He snatched it up. 'Angel.'

'It's Clifton, sir, duty sergeant control room. I've just had an anonymous call from a man who said he'd seen a light in a room of 22 Jubilee Park Road in the early hours of this morning. That's the house where you were recently investigating the murder of an elderly man, I believe. It's not on my list to be secured any more, and SOCO had reported that they'd finished there. I just thought you might want to know ... before I did anything about it. I was only going to get a patrol car to stop as he was passing and take a look at the outside of the place, try the doors and so on.'

Angel frowned. 'Yes, well, thank you, Bernie. You say you don't know who reported it?'

'It was the usual Mr Anonymous, sir.'

'Right. I'll see to it. Thank you. Leave it with me.'

He replaced the phone and turned back to Flora Carter. He told her what the sergeant had reported and instructed her to go there to see if there was anything amiss.

'Give me a ring and tell me what you find,' he said. 'After all, it could be nothing. Christine Elsworth might have been sleeping there and got up in the night to make a cup of tea, or something.'

'Right, sir.'

'Now, where were we? I know. I want you to contact HMRC to get a better understanding of Christine Elsworth's financial position. I've already seen her accountant, Andrew King. And he did say that she was doing very well.'

'Right, sir,' she said. 'I understand, but I'll have a look at 22 Jubilee Park Road, first.'

Angel nodded and she went out.

He looked at the growing pile of post, reports and letters sitting on his desk. He leaned back in the chair for a moment, wiped his hands over his face and considered whether there was anything else he could do to progress the investigation of the murders. Deciding that there was nothing, he pulled the pile towards the middle of the desk and began with the letter at the top.

It had a circulation slip attached to it and had already been seen by the Chief Constable and Detective Superintendent Harker.

It was from the Deputy Chief Constable of West Yorkshire to his Chief Constable. It began with a cordial personal greeting, then it pointed out that the International Jewellery Fair was being held in Leeds from 14 to 19 May and it went on to say that ...

As the Fair organizers are employing their own security company, my force will not supply uniformed presence in or around the premises. Nevertheless, the force will be on hand to deal with conventional attempts at stealing, by pilfering, product substitution and other similar methods by one or more unarmed persons, as well as attempts at major hauls by small armed gangs. However, as a preventive measure, I would ask for your assistance by bringing this Fair to the attention of your officers and asking them to advise me of the presence of any known thieves surfacing in your area both before and during the course of the Fair so that they can be identified, warned, marked by us and tracked by our officers.

Angel remembered reading that the jewellery fair was coming to Leeds. He had not noted the date. The letter advised that it was coming in five days' time. He recalled the old adage: Doesn't time fly?

He wrinkled his nose and thought a moment. The jewellery fair would certainly be an attraction to crooks, but he couldn't say that he'd recognized any of his old clients sniffing around Bromersley of late. But Leeds was twenty miles away. He didn't think it likely that crooks would assemble in Bromersley. Then he recalled that Lord Tulliver lived at Marlborough House, Tunistone, which was only a few miles away, and that the Tullivers were opening the Fair on the first day and that Lady Tulliver would be wearing the fabulous Mermaid Diamond. That jewel alone would tempt many would-be thieves to try to come up with some imaginative idea to get round the strategies of the private security firm, the police and the insurance company.

He had no information to give to the West Yorkshire force, so he ticked his name on the circulation card and rang for Ahmed.

'This needs to go to Inspector Asquith urgently, Ahmed,' he said, handing him the letter.

'Right, sir. And I've just finished checking off Nancy Quinn's mobile phone, if you would like me to—'

Angel's face brightened. 'Oh yes, lad. Bring the list in. It's very important.'

Ahmed had listed the telephone number, person called (where known), date, time and length of each call made from Nancy Quinn's mobile over the last two weeks of her life.

Angel looked at the list. It was surprisingly short.

'Some calls were to Christine Elsworth, sir,' Ahmed said. 'Some to the flower kiosk, several were to her mobile and several to her home address. She made a lot of calls to shops. It seems that she was always buying clothes by phone.'

Angel knew that to be true. Her flat had been bursting with them.

'Were there any calls made that you were unable to identify?' Angel said.

'Yes, sir. Sixteen, all to the same number. I've marked it in red.'

'Sixteen?' Angel said. '07763193880. Who do you phone that frequently, Ahmed?'

'Dunno, sir.'

'Someone you are worried about, someone who owes you money or somebody you love.'

'But she didn't ring that number the two days before she died, sir,' Ahmed said.

Angel said sombrely, 'Aye. That will be because she had no need to. Her lover – and murderer – was living with her.'

Ahmed's jaw dropped. 'You mean that that number is the number of her murderer, sir?'

'I believe so, Ahmed,' he said. 'It makes sense, doesn't it? And that's the tall man described as having dark hair and a babyface.'

'Wow. She made about two calls most days to him. I have been through to the phone company and all they could tell me was that it was a live line and that it was a pay as you go phone.'

Angel frowned, ran his hand over his mouth and said, 'If we could find someone else who has also spoken to him on that number. It might be possible to catch up with him.'

'How can we do that, sir?'

Still frowning, Angel said slowly, 'I don't know, Ahmed. I really don't know. Leave it with me. I'll give it some thought.'

The phone rang. It was Flora Carter. She sounded strange.

'I'm at Piddington's house, sir, 22 Jubilee Park Road. A lot of damage has been done here; there's rubble everywhere. I don't understand it.'

'Well, force an entry and have a closer look.'

'You don't understand, sir. I'm already inside the house, and the front door wasn't locked. Inside is a mess. Like squatters have been. I think you'll want to see this for yourself.'

Angel stopped the BMW outside the late Mr Piddington's house. He noticed a FOR SALE board in the garden which had not been there before.

He ran up the garden path. He had been concerned about Flora Carter's safety. As he drove from the station, it occurred to him that intruders might still be in the house.

The front door was opened from the inside by Flora Carter.

'Have you checked all the rooms, Flora?' he said.

'Oh yes, sir. There's nobody here now, sir, if that's what you were thinking.'

He stepped inside the house and was amazed by what he saw. Some of the internal walls had holes big enough to put your hand and arm through into the next room or hallway. The floors in the hall and rooms were covered with rubble, broken red bricks, old grey mortar, fragments of faded wallpaper, some stuck to plaster, and grey dust. He looked into the sitting room, which still had its table, sideboard, settee and armchairs, but now with the walls full of holes and the furniture a floor laden with grey dust. Mr Piddington's wheelchair was on its side covered in grey dust. He went all over the house. It was all the same.

'Did you find any tools? This sort of damage must have been made by tools such as picks and hammers … or stone chisels and hammers.'

'No, sir,' she said. 'There are no tools or anything like that. In fact, there is just the furniture. What's the explanation? What were they looking for?'

Angel pursed his lips. 'Oh, yes. He or she or they were looking for something all right. I wonder what Mrs Elsworth can tell us. Better get her here straightaway, Flora. Phone the shop. Then pop round to the neighbours. Somebody's bound to have seen or heard something. I'll just take another look around here.'

'Right, sir,' she said.

Ten minutes later, Christine Elsworth arrived. She was shocked when she saw the state of the house. She went from room to room, her mouth open, her head shaking in disbelief, striding over piles of rubble, treading on bits of broken brick or mortar.

Angel waited for her in the hall.

When she came downstairs, she came across to Angel and said, 'I don't understand it, Inspector. It was all right when I left it yesterday afternoon, after I had shown the estate agent round.'

'You locked the door?'

'Yes, I locked it myself.'

'And what did you do with the key?'

'I gave it to Adrian Potter. He's the estate agent, of Ernest Potter and Son, Victoria Road.'

'But DS Carter found the front door unlocked.'

Christine Elsworth gasped as she heard the news. Then her lip quivered as her hand went to her face.

Angel frowned, then said, 'What's the matter?'

She shook her head. She was unwilling or unable to tell him.

Angel rubbed his chin and said, 'I understand. The other key was with Nancy Quinn and is now in the possession of the man who murdered her.'

She nodded.

'And do you know who that is?' he said.

She swallowed, found her voice and said, 'No. Of course not. If I knew that, Inspector, I would tell you.'

He wasn't so sure that she would. He ran his hand through his hair and said, 'I noticed that the damage is only to the non-load-bearing walls. Do you know why that might be?'

She frowned. 'No idea,' she said.

'I think it is because he was looking for something. Something he expected to find bricked up in a wall. Now, what would he be looking for?'

'I've no idea.'

'Will he come back?'

She shuddered, and her eyes shone like car headlights. She looked away. 'How should I know? I sincerely hope not,' she said. Then quickly she added, 'I must get back to the shop, Inspector. We sometimes get busy at lunchtime. You must excuse me.'

Angel saw that she was terrified. He watched her scurry towards the door.

'Mrs Elsworth,' he said, 'don't worry about the house tonight. We'll get the key from Adrian Potter, lock up and return the key to you at the flower shop, if that's all right with you?' he said.

She stopped, turned, sighed and said, 'Oh, yes. Thank you, Inspector. Thank you very much.'

As she went through the front door, Flora came in and closed it. She looked after her and said, 'She seems in a hurry.'

'She's scared to death, Flora. Too scared to say what she knows. Did you find out anything?'

'Nobody saw or heard anything, sir.'

Angel shook his head. His face muscles tightened. 'Amazing,' he said. 'Well, we'll have to do it the hard way. Do you have a long measuring tape in your kit?'

'It's in my car boot, sir. Do you want me to get it?'

'And have you a pad of graph paper?'

She frowned. 'The sort we use for in road accidents ... to show the position of vehicles, skid marks and so on?'

'That's the stuff,' he said. 'Get it.'

She nodded and dashed out to her car.

When she returned, they measured the outside walls of the house and then the inside measurements, allowing between twenty-seven and twenty-eight centimetres for the thickness of the external walls and between fifteen and sixteen centimetres for internal walls. Then, in the hall at the bottom of the stairs on a small table, Angel drew a plan neatly on the graph paper and, to his dismay, the sums were correct. Using the same system, they measured upstairs and found these sums were also correct.

Angel wrinkled his nose. He had expected to find a discrepancy of a metre or so, that would indicate the presence of a false wall, but it was clearly not so. As he finished winding in the tape, he handed it to Flora and said, 'I'll have another think about this. In the meantime, go to Potter, the estate agents on Victoria Road, and get the key for this place, so that we can lock it up. I'll stay here and wait for you.'

'Right, sir,' Flora said and she went out.

Angel stood in the hall, and rubbed his chin. He heard the front door close. He picked his way through the debris on the stairs, climbed to the top and then stood on the landing amidst broken bricks and mortar and stared up at the wooden rectangle in the ceiling, the entrance to the loft. He knew there should be a pole somewhere around to gain access. He could see nothing of it anywhere in the corners of the landing walls. He saw the airing cupboard and tried to open the door. He had to kick rubble away from the front of it so that it would open, to reveal a smooth, brown wooden pole with a brass hook that fell out into his hands. Behind it was the cistern and several shelves of bedclothes and towels.

With the pole, he was able to reach up to the loft door, open it and unhook the aluminium steps so that they came rattling down to the floor of the landing, ending at his feet. He tested them and they seemed perfectly safe, so he climbed up through the loft door all the way to the top. He had come prepared with a torch and he shone it around. There were networks of spiders' webs of different sizes draped at the far end of the area and behind him, and it was strange to be looking through them at the underside of the roof slates, wooden beams and cross members. Looking downwards, the bedroom and bathroom ceilings seemed to be well covered with insulating material to a thickness of about fifteen centimetres, and he could see three metres away what looked like a lagged water tank and a pipe leading from it also lagged with brown insulating material. There was nothing else in the loft. It all looked very proper and he was about to return down the steps when it occurred to him that, although there was a plethora of spiders' webs throughout the loft area, there were none actually around the loft door and between him and the water tank. That suggested that there might have been a human presence in the loft recently. He pursed his lips. Of course, it could just have been a plumber checking the tank.

Before he could stop himself, he had gingerly made his way across the top of the fibreglass insulation material on the beams to the water tank. He shone the torch onto the top of the tank and turned back the insulation. He found that it was covered with a wooden lid. He removed the lid and shone his torch inside. There was not a drop of water in sight. Instead, at the top, he saw a plastic Yogi Bear mask. Underneath it were many bundles of £20 notes wrapped in see-through wrappers. His pulse began to bang away. His mind was in overdrive. He knew he'd found what he had been looking for and possibly the motive for the murders. It was not a water tank at all, but a large wooden crate. It must have been made in situ because it would have been too big to pass through the loft door. As he fished through it, he discovered that there were £5, £10 as well as £20 notes, each denomination wrapped tightly in cellophane packets of £1,000. A packet of £20 notes straight from the Mint took up little space, and so he found that it was impossible to estimate the amount of the find, except that it must run into millions. He moved the Yogi Bear mask carefully to one side to enable him to pull out a token packet of £1,000 in £20 notes, which he stuffed into his pocket, replaced the lid and the loose insulation on the wooden case, and came down the steps. With the pole, he pushed the aluminium steps back up to the landing ceiling and then pulled down the loft door. As he put the pole back in the cistern cupboard, he wondered where the missing water tank for the house was located, and then, he looked upwards, above the shelves of bedding and towels. The water tank was there, located above the cistern. Simple. Only a plumber would be likely to realize that the camouflaged wooden box in the loft did not contain water.

As he stood on the landing amidst the rubble, he heard the front door close with a bang.

It was Flora Carter. 'It's me, sir,' she called. 'Are you there?'

He came down the stairs.

She waved the key at him and said, 'I've got it, sir.'

His face shone. 'Good. So have I,' he said, and he told her about the find, showed her the packet of £20 notes and said, 'The Yogi Bear mask and the old picture of the Queen indicate that the money is from a big bank robbery from the local Royal Westminster Bank, in 1983. There were three robbers on that job, and all three were wearing Yogi Bear masks.'

Flora's eyes twinkled with excitement. 'Wow, what a find.'

'Yes,' he said. 'But I want you to keep it absolutely shtum. Two men served time for it, while the third – it now looks as if he was the late Mr Piddington – got away scot-free. We might be able to find out who knows about this if we keep it to ourselves for a little while.'

'Right, sir.'

'Now what I want you to do is to get a duplicate of this house key made ASAP. The quickest way would be at that little cobbler's and key-cutter's on Almsgate.'

'Right, sir. What for?'

'I'll tell you when you get back. Now fly!'

She grinned and rushed off.

Angel reached out for his phone and was soon in conversation with the manager of the local branch of the Royal Westminster Bank.

'Are you making any progress in finding out who is passing that old money?' Rodney Ballantyne said.

'I think you might say yes to that, Mr Ballantyne,' Angel said. 'But I need your assistance regarding the history of the case. I need to know the details of the two robbers who were caught, and the result of the court case.'

'That's no problem, Inspector. I'll get all that emailed to you within the hour, if that would be all right?'

'Excellent. Look forward to it, and thank you.'

'It's a pleasure, Inspector, and good luck.'

Angel cancelled the call, then tapped in another number.

'National Crime Operations Faculty,' a voice said. 'Which department do you want?'

'This is DI Angel of Bromersley force,' he said. 'I would like to speak urgently to someone in the electronic surveillance equipment department …'

ELEVEN

Angel parked the BMW on Main Street in the town centre. He looked at his watch. It was 4.30. He got out of the car, rushed down the busy street to the corner on Market Street to Christine Elsworth's flower kiosk.

The girl behind the counter recognized him and said, 'Hello. Mrs Elsworth is in the back....'

Christine Elsworth peered round the doorway behind the counter. She didn't look pleased. 'Oh, it's you, Inspector. Come on through.'

'Thank you,' he said, and he followed her into the small work-room where she was busy cutting a piece of Oasis to fit a metal frame intended to support a floral display.

Angel said, 'I thought you'd like to know ... I have locked up the house and and here's the key.' He fished around in his pocket, found it and handed it to her.

'Thank you,' she said. 'Did you find anything at all helpful there?'

'I'm afraid not,' he lied. He rubbed his jaw. 'I cannot for the life of me see what the intruder was looking for.'

'I've been thinking who I can get to make good the damage.'

'You can probably claim on your insurance, and I would have thought your estate agent would be able to advise on that.'

'Of course. I must ask him.'

Angel pursed his lips. 'Those holes in the walls made me think that the intruder must have been looking for something ... something really valuable. I have had a good look round and I couldn't find anything, anything at all. Have you any idea what it was? Did your father keep any jewellery in the house ... or a stockpile of sovereigns ... or a big pile of cash?'

'Not to my knowledge, Inspector,' she said. 'If he had, it would have turned up by now, wouldn't it? My father only had his pension and it was a struggle every week to pay all his bills, keep him cared for, warm and well fed. I invariably had to contribute something to keep him going. Not that I minded. He kept *me* going when *I* was in trouble. He kept me together when my husband died.'

Angel nodded sympathetically. 'Even so, Mrs Elsworth, there must be a reason why someone would make holes in the walls like that.'

'Well, Inspector, I'm sorry, I have no idea what it was.'

'Right, well, if anything occurs to you, give me a ring. Good afternoon.'

'I certainly will, Inspector. Good afternoon.'

He came out of the kiosk and back round the corner to the BMW. He started the engine and pointed the bonnet in the direction of Victoria Road, the long street of offices. He soon found Ernest Potter and Son and went through the glass door and up to the counter. A young woman was tapping something out on a computer keyboard. She turned and looked up at him.

'I want to speak to Mr Potter, Adrian Potter, please,' he said. 'I am DI Angel.'

'I'm Adrian Potter,' a voice behind him said. He had followed him through the internal door. 'I was just leaving, Inspector. But if I can help you ...'

'Can we go somewhere where we can talk?' Angel said.

He noticed that Potter blinked nervously, as he said, 'Of course. Please follow me.'

Potter made his way out of the reception area, through another door into a small, tidy little office.

Angel followed him, looking round at all the different photographs of houses and properties on the wall.

Potter pointed to the chair in front of the desk, while he sat down behind it. 'Now, Inspector, what's it all about?'

'You have been instructed by Mrs Christine Elsworth to sell a house?'

'Yes, 22 Jubilee Park Road.'

'You had a key to the place? Mrs Elsworth gave it to you late yesterday afternoon?'

'Yes. A police sergeant, a very pretty woman, took it from me this morning. I have her name and number in the key book. I hope that was on the level.'

'Yes. That was my sergeant. And I have just returned the key to Mrs Elsworth.'

Potter frowned. 'If I am expected to sell the property, Inspector, the key should be here in this office at all times for prospective buyers to be able to see over the place.'

'I'm sure you're right, but perhaps you could sort that out with Mrs Elsworth?'

'I certainly will, but what's your interest, Inspector?'

'Well, I need to know the names and addresses of the people who have expressed interest in the place.'

'Well, nobody has actually had the key, Inspector. It is early days. Nor has it been advertised in the papers yet. I believe there has only been just the one phone call. I remember speaking to somebody yesterday about it. My secretary may have fielded some other enquiries while I was out.'

He picked up the phone and said, 'Jane, have you had any enquiries at all re 22 Jubilee Park Road? ... Nothing? ... Oh?'

Potter's eyebrows shot up.

Angel watched him attentively.

'Of course,' Potter continued into the phone. 'Yes. I remember now ... yes ... right.'

He replaced the receiver, turned to Angel and said, 'She reminded me that there was a standing enquiry for anything near or around the park from a Mr Oliver.'

Angel frowned.

'There's nothing wrong, is there?'

'No, sir. There's nothing wrong.'

'I will be able to continue to offer it for sale, won't I? It's in a popular area, near the park, and on the fringe of a better class of architect-designed homes. Although the market is very depressed, I would expect to sell it fairly quickly.'

'I don't see why not. Again, you'll need to sort that out with Mrs Elsworth. Now will you let me have the two names and addresses?'

'Certainly,' Potter said, opening a drawer. 'It's here, in my book.' He took out a large property book and turned over some pages. 'Here we are, 22 Jubilee Park Road. He read out his notes. '9/5/13, Charles Morris, the Old Vicarage, St Peter's Close, Tunistone, phoned requesting full details and price.'

Angel was not surprised to hear that name. He was still awaiting a report on that man from Trevor Crisp. He must remember to put a squib up Crisp's backside. He took out the old envelope from his inside pocket and made a note of Morris's address.

Potter then turned back to the first page in the property book. 'And this is the name and phone number of the standing enquirer interested in any property in or near Jubilee Park, Mr Edward

Oliver. He phoned originally on 6/5/13. Only means of contact, by mobile phone.'

Angel's eyebrows shot up. That was suspicious in itself, he reckoned as he licked his bottom lip. Edward Oliver was a name he had not come across in this inquiry. Heat began to generate in his chest and increased as he scribbled away. There *was* another suspect.

'I phoned him yesterday,' Potter said. 'I told him I had this house to offer and he sounded interested. He said he would drop into the office when he was next in town.'

Angel's heart was thumping. 'And what was his number?'

'07763193880,' Potter said.

As Angel scribbled the number down, his chest was burning and throbbing. He now had three suspects when up till then he had had only one. Things were looking up.

As he looked at the number the more he thought he had recently come across it before. The double seven at the beginning and the double eight at the end seemed familiar. He eagerly turned his envelope over, searching for the number. He found it. It was there. It *was* the same number; it was identical to the one Nancy Quinn had rung frequently on her mobile the last two weeks of her life except for the last two days. For those two days, Angel reckoned, the owner of the number, Edward Oliver, was living with her in her flat and it was he who eventually, madly, crazily stabbed her to death while they were apparently making love.

Angel reached into his pocket and took out his business card. He put it down in front of Potter and said, 'I would be pleased if you would kindly let me know if Edward Oliver makes any further approach to you.'

'Oh yes, Inspector,' Potter said. 'I didn't know you knew him. What sort of a man is he?'

'Interesting,' Angel said. 'Very interesting.'

He came out of Potter's office, got into the BMW. He was quite excited now that he had the name of the murderer. He looked at the dashboard clock. It was 5.15. So he drove straight home.

He put the car in the garage, and went down the path to the back door. He let himself in with his key, closed the door and looked round the kitchen. There was no sign of Mary and no sign of tea. He was about to call out when he heard her rushing from the hall to the kitchen with a magazine in her hand. She had a big smile on her face.

'Hello, darling,' she said. 'I thought I heard the door. What are you doing here?'

He frowned. 'I live here,' he said.

'No, no,' she said with a laugh and gave him a quick peck on the cheek. 'I mean you're so early. You're never as early as this.'

'I am sometimes. I finish at five,' he said.

'I know. I know. Well, I'm sorry. Tea isn't ready. I didn't expect you for another half hour or so.'

'That's all right, sweetheart,' he said. 'There's no rush.'

'But you've come just in time,' she said and she thrust the magazine she was holding into his hand and said, 'What's the answer to question nine? It's for a winter cruise round the Norwegian fjords. You'll know it. You have that sort of memory.'

He wrinkled his nose and held up the magazine. 'You always said you didn't want to go anywhere cold for a holiday. And there's nowhere colder than the Norwegian fjords in winter.'

'Never mind all that, Michael. It's *free!*'

'Free? So what? I wouldn't go on a holiday I didn't want to go on simply because it was free.'

'There are other prizes,' she said, then she snatched back the magazine, glanced at the question and said, '"What is the name of the Greek goddess of love and beauty?" Do you know it?'

He smiled. 'Of course I know it. The Greek goddess of love and beauty is Mary,' he said boldly and with a deadpan expression. 'Now, how about something to eat?'

Mary looked at him and frowned. Her mouth opened slightly. She licked her pretty lips. 'I know that Venus is the *Roman* goddess of love and beauty ... and I was pretty certain that the Greek was Aphrodite.'

'It's Mary, definitely,' he said. He turned away to avoid her eyes. 'Now, what's for tea?'

'I just want to finish this,' she said, still frowning and trying to catch his eye. 'Are you sure it's Mary?'

'If you've put Aphrodite, your name won't even be in the hat. You'll ruin any chance of going up to the North Pole.'

Her eyes flashed. 'It isn't the North Pole, it's the Norwegian fjords.'

'Well, Mary, I ask you. Do you really want to go to the Norwegian fjords in the middle of winter?'

She hesitated. 'If it's free, I suppose ... well, I wouldn't mind. They say it's breathtaking.'

'I think you've misread it.'

She looked at him indignantly. 'I have not misread it. Give me credit for being able to read.'

'No. You've misread it. It says that it's freezing, not that it's free!'

Her eyebrows went up, then came down as she looked at him closely.

He couldn't contain himself any longer. He had to smile.

She saw him and broke into a laugh.

The game was up.

He guffawed, then said, 'I mean ... I mean ... whoever heard of Mary at the waterhole?'

'I knew it was Aphrodite all the time,' she said. 'You rotten tease.'

'What did you ask me for, then?'

'I just needed confirmation, that's all.'

They had a good giggle, then Mary turned away to the fridge, opened the door and took out a packet of smoked salmon, eggs, butter and milk. 'If you set the table, Michael, tea will be ready in five minutes.'

'Thank you, darling,' he said, giving her a gentle kiss on the lips.

He took out a beer from the fridge and a tumbler from the cupboard and poured himself a glass of his favourite German beer.

They had smoked salmon and scrambled egg, one of Angel's favourite meals. And when they had settled in the sitting room with coffee, Mary said, 'You seem in a good mood tonight, Michael, is there some particular reason?'

'Oh, well … it's coming home to you at the end of the day,' he said.

She kissed him on the forehead. 'I don't believe a word of it,' she said, smiling.

He smiled back and squeezed her hand.

'No,' she continued. 'Something has happened at work. Er … you've solved the case? You've got the murderer?'

'You're partly right, sweetheart. We have got the murderer's name.'

'Oh? That's great, isn't it?'

'It would be if I knew where to find him.'

'What's his name?'

'Edward Oliver.'

'Edward Oliver? Which one is he? Where does he fit in? I've not heard you mention *him* before.'

'I don't know myself. We have his mobile number, and we have two independent witnesses who have given us descriptions of the man which are pretty well in agreement.'

She smiled. 'That's why you're looking like the cat that got the cream.'

'Well, we've still got to find the man,' he said. 'That's the first thing – no, the second thing I must see to in the morning.'

Mary blinked. 'Why, what's the first?'

'There's a video recorder with a night lens, set up in the attic of old Mr Piddington's house. There is a hoard of paper money hidden up there, enough to constitute a motive. I want to see who knows about it. It could be our Mr Edward Oliver.'

TWELVE

It was 9 a.m. on Friday, 10 May 2013.

There was a knock on the door. 'Come in,' Angel said.

Flora entered with a black metal box the size of a cigar box, with a length of connecting cable wrapped round it.

'Good morning, sir,' she said.

'Come in, lass,' he said.

'You'll not be surprised to hear that all the money is gone,' she said.

'Not at all. It's worth it, if it's all recorded on that videotape. You've got it?'

'Yes, sir, and there's the front door key,' she said, putting a shiny new key on his desk.

Angel picked it up and put it in his pocket.

'How long has the tape run for?'

'Looks like more than an hour, sir.'

He looked pleased. He swung round in the swivel chair to the table behind, picked up his laptop and gave it to her. 'Can you set it up and let's see what we've got?'

Flora began the business of linking the video to the laptop with a cable and finding a mains power socket in which to plug the laptop.

Angel said, 'Did you see anything of a Yogi Bear mask in Piddington's attic?'

'No, sir. But I do remember you did say something about it being with the money. I expect Christine Elsworth took it.'

'There might be good prints on it,' he said. 'Provide evidence of the robbery.'

They both looked at the laptop screen. It was pitch black.

'It's running, sir. I hope it's working,' she said.

'It records when there is enough light,' he said. 'And it has a night lens, so it should be OK.'

A clock face suddenly appeared on the screen informing them that the time was 02.06 hours, Friday, 10 May 2013. That was followed by a flashing picture of Piddington's attic, depicting the underside of the roof tiles, the wooden beams, the cobwebs and the camouflaged water tank.

The ever-moving light source seemed to be a flashlight. A human figure carrying something bulky came into view from the bottom of the picture. It covered the video camera lens briefly. The figure then moved towards the wooden case and disposed of whatever it had been carrying out of range of the picture. The figure then seemed to be trying to find an appropriate position for the flashlight, first placing it on the edge of the wooden case where it fell into it. The figure then leaned inside to retrieve it when for the first time the head turned to the camera and as the light was brought out of the case it was possible for Angel and Flora Carter to see the face of the figure in the picture was a woman.

'Mrs Elsworth,' they said in unison.

Angel was shocked. He shook his head and wrinkled his nose. 'His own daughter,' he said.

'Did Christine Elsworth murder her own father, sir?'

'Well, she had the means, the opportunity and now *there's* the motive. But, we have still to prove it,' he said. 'There are some prints on the back of the wheelchair that have not yet been identified. Don Taylor is trying to match them up.'

They both stared at the laptop screen.

Christine Elsworth was bending up and down over the packing case. She worked quickly and energetically. The explanation for her movements became clear. She was transferring the money into sacks. When she had filled a sack sufficiently, she tied a knot in the neck of it and dropped it through the loft door. The operation was repeated many times. Angel sped up the replay until they saw her put the cover over the packing case and leave the loft. When the flashlight went down through the loft door, the camera stopped rolling and the recording stopped.

He switched off the laptop, turned back to his desk and looked across it at Flora. 'The first thing is to get a warrant for the arrest of Christine Elsworth for handling stolen money.'

Flora frowned. 'What about the charge of murdering her father?' she said.

'We would look like awful berks if we were wrong about that, whereas we know for certain that she has handled the stolen money. We can add a murder charge when we have proof.'

'Right, sir,' she said.

'Then liaise with Don Taylor. I want a full search of her house, her car and the flower shop, obviously for the money, but also for that Yogi Bear mask which I want you to handle as little as possible and bag for SOCO; hopefully they'll find prints.'

'Right, sir,' she said and made for the door.

He called after her. 'By the way, didn't I ask you to contact HMRC and make surreptitious enquiries into her accounts?'

Her eyes opened wide and her jaw dropped. 'Yes, sir,' she said. 'That was only yesterday morning. When have I had the time to—'

'I know, Flora. I know,' he said, waving a hand. 'I'm not chasing you. As soon as you can, lass. I only wanted to say that now, the enquiries need not be at all surreptitious.'

'Oh yes. I see. I'll get to it … eventually … I hope.'

He watched her leave and the door close before he allowed himself to smile after her.

He reached out for the phone. 'Ahmed,' he said. 'Come on in here.'

'Yes, sir,' Ahmed said.

Angel replaced the phone.

Ahmed knocked on his office door and entered. He had a few loose sheets of A4 in his hand. 'Good morning, sir.'

'There are a few jobs I want you to do for me, lad,' Angel said.

'Before you start, sir, can I give you these notes? They came by email from the Royal Westminster Bank, and they are about that bank robbery in Bromersley in 1983.'

Angel frowned, then brightened as he remembered. 'Right, lad. Thank you. Put them down there,' he said quickly. 'I'll see to them later. I've a lot on my mind and I don't want to forget anything. Right, now firstly, I want you to find DS Crisp and tell him I want him. Secondly I want you to get me that reel-to-reel recorder. I want to make a phone call and make a recording of it. And thirdly, I want you to go onto the PNC and see if you can find any record of a villain called Edward Oliver. He lives somewhere in Yorkshire, Lincolnshire or Derbyshire, I think. If you can't find him on the PNC, try the telephone directories. All right?'

'Right, sir,' Ahmed said and then ran out.

Angel picked up the phone. He tapped in a single digit for the SOCO office. Taylor answered.

'Now then, Don, about the prints on the back of the wheelchair, have you found out whose they are?'

'No, sir. They've been checked off against all the prints I have. But, you know, I haven't seen the prints of Moira Elsworth nor her boyfriend, Charles Morris.'

Angel pursed his lips. 'Why not? I interviewed the girl on

Tuesday, and asked her to call in here ASAP and bring him with her.'

'They haven't been here, sir.'

Angel breathed in and out heavily. 'All right, Don,' he said. 'Leave it with me, I'll have to chase them.'

There was a knock on the door.

'Come in,' Angel said as he replaced the phone.

It was DS Crisp. 'Ahmed said you wanted me, sir.'

Angel's top lip tightened back against his teeth. 'Of course I want you. I wish I didn't. I gave you a simple enquiry the day before yesterday and I've not heard a word from you. Where've you been, lad, Moscow?'

'No, sir. I've had a terrible job. The Charles Morris ... the one with that National Insurance number you gave me, is dead.'

Angel frowned. 'Dead?'

Crisp pulled out a folded piece of paper. He opened it up. 'This is a copy of his death certificate. He died last November in a hospital in Hull of hepatitis and pneumonia, aged forty-two.'

He passed it over to Angel. He took it and read it carefully, then rubbed his chin.

'He's not known at HMRC,' Crisp said. 'And Work and Pensions have him down as sign-writer for a firm in Hull, but made redundant in May last year. The NHS have him down as single and living in Stanley Road, Hull, which is the same address given by Work and Pensions and the council tax office in Hull town hall.'

'That sounds pretty conclusive,' Angel said. 'Right, Trevor. Good work. The question now is, who is the man with a six pack in Tunistone, parading about as a man about town?'

'Don't know, sir. But it isn't Charles Morris.'

'Very well, Trevor. Bring him in for questioning, and do it straightaway.'

'Right, sir.'

*

There was a knock at the door. It was Flora Carter.

'I've got Mrs Elsworth and her solicitor in interview room number one, sir.'

Angel stood up. 'Right, Flora, who is her solicitor?'

'A man called Gerald Mackenzie.'

Angel shook his head as he crossed the little office and made for the door. 'Never heard of him.'

They went down the corridor and Angel said, 'Is Don Taylor getting on with searching Christine Elsworth's house?'

'He said he would get on with it straightaway,' she said, 'and phone you on your mobile if they find the money.'

They reached the interview room to find PC Leisha Baverstock on the door.

'Good morning, sir,' she said with a big smile.

Angel nodded and smiled back. 'Don't let anybody interrupt us, Leisha.'

'Right, sir.'

Angel and Flora Carter went in.

Christine Elsworth and Gerald Mackenzie were seated at the interview table. Mackenzie stood up and came across to Angel and held out his hand to shake it.

'Pleased to meet you, Inspector. I'm Gerald Mackenzie. I'm representing Mrs Elsworth.'

Angel shook his hand. He had a warm, strong grip that Angel liked. 'Good morning, Mr Mackenzie.'

He then looked across at Mrs Elsworth and smiled and nodded. She raised her nose and lowered the corners of her mouth, then turned away.

Angel had the uncomfortable feeling that she really could have murdered her own father.

Flora took the seat opposite Mackenzie and Angel sat opposite Mrs Elsworth.

Angel switched on the recording machine and rattled through the obligatory introduction, then began the questioning.

'Mrs Elsworth, what do you know about a large quantity of stolen paper money concealed in the loft of your late father's house, number 22 Jubilee Park Road?'

Christine Elsworth's eyes shone and her mouth dropped open. The question had astounded her. There were several seconds before she said, 'I don't know anything about it.'

Angel's eyebrows dropped and he rubbed his chin.

Mackenzie whispered something into her ear.

'I mean I knew it was there,' she said, 'but I didn't know how it *got* there.'

'You didn't know that your father with others had stolen it from a bank?' Angel said.

'No.'

'Where did you think the money had come from, then?'

'I don't know. I really have no idea.'

'There were ten million pounds in your father's attic and you had no idea how it got there?'

'No idea.'

'And is that all you have to say on the matter?'

'I took it for granted that if it was in my father's attic, it must have been his.'

Angel ran a hand through his hair.

'Ten million pounds,' he said. 'Why? Did you think that your mother had saved it out of the housekeeping?'

Flora smiled.

Mrs Elsworth looked furious and stared at Mackenzie.

Mackenzie said, 'Really, Inspector. That's a very improper question.'

'Very well,' Angel said. 'I will withdraw it, if you will get your client to treat my questions seriously and answer them truthfully.'

Mackenzie and Mrs Elsworth exchanged whispers.

Angel rubbed his chin and waited until they had finished, then said, 'All right, I'll try it another way. Did you think that the money in your father's loft had been attained by hard work and honest toil?'

'I don't know,' she said.

Angel wrinkled his nose. 'What was your father's job?'

'He was a tyre fitter in a garage.'

'A tyre fitter in a garage ... that's not a very highly paid job, is it?'

'I don't know.'

'There's a lot you don't know, Mrs Elsworth,' he said, then he shrugged and shook his head. He pursed his lips, thought a moment, then said, 'Mrs Elsworth, how long have you known that there was all that money in your father's loft?'

She frowned. 'Not very long,' she said.

'Well, it has been there for thirty years. How long are we talking about? Twenty years, ten years, two years?'

'About six weeks,' she said.

'I understand that your father suffered from a form of amnesia during the last few months of his life.'

'So he did,' she said, 'most of the time. But he managed to talk to me sensibly one day. He told me that there were thousands and thousands of pounds in the loft and that if anything was to happen to him I was to take it. It was for me.'

'Didn't you ask him how much there was, and how he had come by it?'

'I did. But he had gone back into the fog by that time.'

Angel breathed in and then noisily breathed out. 'Did you ever take any of the money and spend it at any time?'

'No. I have never considered the money mine even though it was left to me by my father.'

131

'So you left it there, concealed in the loft?'

She hesitated. 'Yes.'

'And it is *still* there?'

'Yes, as far as I know,' she said.

Angel shook his head and rubbed his chin. If lying were an Olympic sport, Christine Elsworth would have been awarded a bag of gold medals.

His mobile rang. He took it out of his pocket, pressed a button, read the LCD and saw that it was Don Taylor.

'Excuse me,' he said and turned away.

'Yes, Don,' he said into the mouthpiece. 'Yes … yes … how many? … You're certain? … Thank you, Don. 'Bye.'

He turned back to face Christine Elsworth. 'So, you were saying that, as far as you knew, the money concealed in the loft, is still there.'

She stared hard at him and said, 'Yes.'

Angel said, 'You've been keeping something back from me, Mrs Elsworth, haven't you?'

'No,' she said. Her face was straight, tight-lipped and defiant. 'I've answered all your questions.'

'That is so, yes. But you neglected to tell me about your twin sister.'

She frowned, then said, 'But I haven't got a twin sister.'

'That's strange,' he said. 'Because somebody who looked just like you cleared out all the money from the loft in your father's house at just after two o'clock this morning. She put the money in twenty black plastic bags and – of all the cheek! – hid them in the cellar in *your* house.'

Christine Elsworth went red and then purple. She turned to Mackenzie, who looked confused. Some fervent whispering ensued.

Angel quietly turned away.

*

At that morning's sitting of the magistrates' court, Christine Elsworth was summoned to attend the crown court on a date to be determined, charged with handling the money, with bail set in her own recognizance at £5,000. The magistrates also issued a court order for possession of the stolen money.

Angel came out of the court with the chief clerk to the court, solicitor Mr Cresswell, and the CPS barrister, Mr Twelvetrees. Both legal eagles agreed that the crown court would find Christine Elsworth guilty when the case was heard later in the year.

Angel made his excuses courteously on the steps of the court and rushed over to his office in the police station. He was pleased to see that Ahmed had brought in the reel-to-reel recorder and put it on his desk. He would have to get to it as soon as he possibly could.

He picked up the phone and tapped in DS Taylor's mobile number. 'Don, when you have checked over those plastic bags of money, I want you to take them to the magistrates' court office. The magistrates have issued a court order for possession of the money, so it will all have to be delivered to the clerk of the court, Alan Cresswell, ASAP. And be sure and get a receipt. All right?'

'Right, sir,' Taylor said.

'Tell me, have you found anything else of interest to us in her house?'

'Only that Yogi Bear mask, which we have carefully bagged. If she's anything to hide, she's made a good job of it.'

'Right, Don. Keep at it.'

Angel returned the phone to its holster. It immediately began to ring. He reached out for it again. It was DS Crisp.

'Yes, lad,' Angel said. 'I was beginning to wonder where you'd got to.'

Crisp sounded breathless. 'It's Charles Morris, sir. He's gone. The flat has been vacated. Apparently he left yesterday, although his rent is paid up to the end of the month.'

Angel was speechless. He was kicking himself for not being quicker in reacting to the man's reluctance to come forward to leave his fingerprints. Morris could be the murderer and Angel had so easily let him slip through his fingers.

'Are you there, sir?' Crisp said.

'How do you know he left yesterday?' Angel said.

'The neighbours told me. They're two old biddies who would never miss anything. They saw him loading his bags and stuff into his car.'

'And how do you know his rent is paid up?'

'The church apparently still owns the old vicarage and lets it out, and the rent is paid monthly to a church warden, Mr Timms, who told me.'

'Mmmm. See what else you can find out about Morris. Ask around the village locals, his neighbours, anybody he might have come into contact with. Morris might have dropped some titbit of information in an unguarded moment.'

'Right, sir. I'll give it a try.'

'I wish we had a photograph of him.'

'He'd be very chary about that, particularly if he's on the run.'

'Aye,' he said thoughtfully. 'Tell you what, Trevor, I'm going to send a fingerprint man up there immediately, so stop anybody going into the flat. Also, find Morris's refuse and guard it with your life until Don Taylor and his lads get up there. Then report back to me. All right?'

Angel then promptly instructed DS Taylor to send a finger-print man to Morris's flat in Tunistone directly, and then for the rest of the SOCO team to join their man in Tunistone as soon as they had finished searching Christine Elsworth's property. He needed to know as much as possible about the mysterious Mr Morris.

He then turned his attention to the reel-to-reel recorder on his desk in front of him. He connected it to his landline phone, switched on the recorder, cleared his throat to check the sound level indicator needle, then he tapped in Edward Oliver's mobile number.

As he listened to the phone ringing out, he felt his mouth go dry and his pulse rate quicken. After all, he was about to speak to a murderer.

A man's voice all of a sudden said, 'Hello?'

'It that Mr Oliver?' Angel said.

'Who wants to know?'

The owner of the voice was fairly well spoken. He was either educated or giving a good imitation of someone who had been educated.

'I understand that you were interested in 22 Jubilee Park Road?'

There was a pause, then the voice said, 'I might be. Who *is* this?'

'I'm speaking for Adrian Potter, estate agents, Ernest Potter and Son, Victoria Road. He wondered if you wanted to view the house?'

'Just a minute,' he said. 'I know who you are. You're that nosey detective who is always getting his name in the papers. The know-all who reckons he hasn't lost a case yet. Detective Inspector Michael Angel, isn't it? Look, Angel, I've given you one warning. And from me, one is enough, I promise you. Keep out of my way.'

'You don't frighten me – whoever you are, just because you murdered a young woman. Why don't you give yourself up? You're obviously sick.'

'You don't understand. And you never will understand. I loved that girl, but she wouldn't tell me where the money was hidden.'

'Maybe that was because she didn't know.'

'*She knew*. Anyway, I am warning you, Angel, keep out of it, or you'll go the same way she did. You'll never catch me.'

'I am only a footstep behind you. Give yourself up before you hurt anybody else.'

'Oh, I'm not scared of you, Angel. Now, this is your last warning. I haven't finished yet and you'll be next if you don't keep out of my way.'

'Huh! I don't think so.'

The line went dead.

Angel knew he had gone. His heart was beating like a Salvation Army drum. He replaced the phone in its holster, ran back the recording and listened to the playback. He was quite disturbed by some of what he heard.

Firstly, he realized that the man recognized him solely from the sound of his voice, therefore he must have heard him speak several times at least. A voice could not be remembered after a short, casual exchange. He must have heard Angel speak at length, perhaps in an interview, or several interviews, or in court. The policeman had interviewed hundreds of witnesses and villains over the years, and been interviewed himself many times in court. It was disturbing. And there was something else: if the murderer knew him, then Angel must know the murderer.

Secondly, there was the threat to keep out of his way or he would murder him. Over the years Angel had had so many threats from all sorts of villains and brushed them aside as merely words. On this occasion, it seemed different.

There was a knock at the door. 'Come in.'

It was Ahmed.

Angel looked up at him.

'I can't find any trace of an Edward Oliver, sir. I've also tried Ted Oliver, T. Oliver, Ed Oliver and Eddie Oliver. I can't find a thing. Do you want me to extend the area or try another name?'

'No, Ahmed, thank you. It is obviously a waste of time.'

'Is Edward Oliver the name of the murderer of Nancy Quinn, sir?'

Angel nodded. 'It's an alias he has used, Ahmed. I'd give anything to know his *real* name. I now have his voice on the recorder. Will you take that machine into the CID office and ask the officers to listen to it? If anybody thinks they recognize the voice I'd be pleased to hear from them.'

'Right, sir.'

Angel stood up and reached out for his coat.

'Oh yes, Ahmed. There's another thing.'

Ahmed reached for his notebook and pen.

'Can you get in touch with Scrivens on his mobile?' Angel said as he pushed an arm through the coat sleeve. 'I've sent him off to get some info on a character called Ronald Arthur Bottomley. Will you tell him that Bottomley was one of the two robbers caught after the big robbery from Royal Westminster Bank in 1983. If he comes across it, the other one's name was Vernon Almond. Got it?'

'Right, sir,' Ahmed said with a knowing look. 'So you managed to get through that email from the bank, then, sir?'

'Aye. I make a point of reading everything to do with the case that is put in front of me, Ahmed. I look at everything and everybody concerned with the case. It's sorting out what's significant to the investigation, and what is not, that's important.'

'Yes, sir,' Ahmed said thoughtfully. 'I see what you mean.'

'I'm going up to Tunistone to Charles Morris's flat. If you want me, you can get me on my mobile.'

THIRTEEN

Angel found the flats easily. He only had to look for a church steeple, to find St Peter's Church, and the old vicarage was only thirty metres away.

The ground floor had only two flats on it and Morris had been living in flat 2. Angel knocked on the door, opened it and looked inside.

DS Taylor in his white paper overalls and four other men dressed similarly looked across at him.

'Oh, it's you, sir,' Taylor said.

Angel nodded.

Taylor came across the big room towards him. The other three SOCO men carried on with the searching operation.

Angel closed the door and looked round. It was a big, sparsely furnished sitting room with French windows both sides of the fireplace which opened out to a long, well-maintained garden. On the chimney breast was hanging an old French clock with a face the size of a dinner plate. It showed the time at 10.58 a.m.

'Got anything of interest, Don?'

Taylor smiled. 'Yes, sir,' he said, 'and I think you'll like it.'

He reached into a large white shoulder bag at his feet, unzipped it, took out a polythene evidence bag and held it up.

Angel could see that the bag contained a plastic Yogi Bear mask, identical to the one he'd found with the money in

Piddington's loft. His pulse began to race. 'Where did you find that?'

'In the wheelie bin, sir. Morris had obviously discarded it.'

Angel smiled. 'That would be another one of the three masks worn during the robbery in 1983, and it lends credence to the hypothesis that Charles Morris knew about Ernest Piddington and the ten million quid. However, it seemed that he didn't know it was sitting in his loft disguised as a water tank.'

'I knew you'd be pleased.'

'Any prints on it?'

'There are some smudges, sir. We haven't had chance to make any comparisons yet. And we haven't been able to pick up any of Charles Morris's fingerprints either.'

Angel looked at him strangely. 'But the man lived here for a few months. Don't tell me he's been eating, sleeping, washing and doing whatever else people do with gloves on?'

'Every surface, ridge, doorknob, door handle, grip and ledge we can think of has been wiped over with a cotton vest soaked in white spirit. It's as if he knew we would be looking for them.'

Angel frowned. 'How do you know it's a vest?'

'Because we found it in the waste, sir. It was at the top of his wheelie.'

Angel wrinkled his nose. 'Is it all right if I walk about the place?'

'Yes, sir. The vacuuming is done, the photography and the floor are finished. All we have to do is a finger search and a final look round for his prints.'

There was a knock at the door.

'Excuse me, sir,' Taylor said, and he went across the room and opened the door.

'Come in, Mr Timms,' Taylor said.

A big man with a face like a worried hippopotamus came in. 'This is most irregular,' Timms said. 'We've never had a tenant who dashed off leaving us with a flat to let like this. It is most irregular. And I'm afraid that he paid his rent in cash.'

Taylor looked disappointed. 'Thank you for checking anyway,' he replied. 'Meet my boss, Detective Inspector Angel. He's in charge of the case. This is Mr Timms, church warden of St Peter's. Mr Timms has been to see how Morris paid his rent. I thought if he had had a bank account, we could possibly have been able to trace him that way.'

Angel nodded. Then he smiled courteously at Timms and said, 'I am sorry that your tenant has run out on you. We are also very interested in catching up with him. Can you tell me? ... When he applied for the tenancy of the flat, how did he hear that it was coming vacant?'

'We ran an advertisement in the *Bromersley Chronicle*,' Timms said.

'And in response to that, he wrote to you?'

'No. He phoned.'

'Did he say where he was living at the time?'

'I believe he said he was staying in a hotel.'

Angel rubbed his chin. 'A hotel? In Bromersley or ... or some other town?'

'I don't believe he said, Inspector. If he did, I don't remember.'

'Mmm.'

The clock on the chimney breast began to strike. Angel looked at his watch. It said 11.05. 'I think it's slow,' he said.

Taylor said, 'Yes, sir. It is.'

Timms looked at his watch. 'Five minutes. Can't abide a slow clock,' he said and went up to the wall to take it down.

Angel said, 'Leave it, sir, please.'

Timms's jaw dropped. 'I just want to put it right, Inspector.'

Angel turned to Taylor. 'Has it been checked for prints, Don?' he said.

'Don't know, sir. We don't usually check stuff on walls like clocks for prints. I'll find out.'

While Taylor rushed off to consult the member of the SOCO team who had been responsible for checking for fingerprints throughout the flat, Angel turned back to the church warden and said, 'Sorry, Mr Timms, for being so abrupt, but we are anxious not to miss any place where this chap Morris's fingerprints might be.'

'That's all right, Inspector. I didn't realize. But you do have to take the clock off the wall to adjust the time. I am used to it. I am afraid it seems to lose about three minutes a week.'

Taylor returned with one of his SOCO team, a young detective constable in white paper overalls and rubber gloves carrying a pot of aluminium powder and a soft brush. The young man deftly applied thin amounts of powder with the brush on the glass and wood face of the clock, and peered at the result from different angles using a small hand torch. Apparently finding nothing usable, he carefully removed the clock from the wall and did the same to the back of the clock. His face brightened when he peered closely at his handiwork with the torch, and he reached into his pocket for a roll of clear tape.

Angel read the signs. 'What you got, lad?' he said.

'Eight fingertips. Four at each side. Must have been made while taking the clock off the wall, sir,' the detective constable said. 'There were corresponding thumb prints on the face of the clock, but they were smudged.'

'Are they recent?'

'They seem to be, sir.'

The young man lifted the prints with the tape and applied the tape to stiff card, then he made some notes on the card, returned the clock to the wall, and went away into another room.

Angel turned to Taylor and said, 'Get him to email those prints to Records immediately, Don.'

'Right, sir.'

Satisfied that the search for the ID of Charles Morris was moving along satisfactorily, Angel left Taylor and his SOCO team at Morris's flat and returned to the station.

He was sitting at his desk trying to make sense of all the details accumulated in the two murder cases. It was difficult trying to distinguish between inconsequential information, and vital, meaningful evidence. He considered the facts. A beautiful young woman, Nancy Quinn, carer to old Mr Piddington, was savagely murdered by stabbing which seemed to have occurred during sexual intercourse. The man known as Edward Oliver boasted as much, and Angel had a description of him from two witnesses. They had said that he was tall, dark and handsome with a cherubic face. In addition, while speaking to him on the phone, Oliver had quickly recognized Angel's voice, which meant he must have known Angel and in turn Angel must know him, at least to have spoken to him several times. However, Angel couldn't bring him to mind. There were so many people he had spoken to over the years.

Then Angel turned his thoughts to the murder of Ernest Piddington.

His first suspect was Piddington's daughter, Christine Elsworth, suspicious because she wanted to keep the existence of the money secret and thereby retain it entirely for herself? Perhaps she was worried that in his ramblings, old Mr Piddington might have let out the secret of the money in the loft to some villain.

His second suspect was the man purporting to be Charles Morris, who was courting Moira Elsworth possibly to get near the money. An individual who had now vanished. Angel had told

Moira that her fingerprints *and* his would be required. When she conveyed the message, Morris seemed to have run off, dumping the 30-year-old mask on the way.

Angel was thinking about that when he recalled that Moira's fingerprints had still not yet been obtained. Also, it was quite possible that she could assist them in their search for Morris.

He reached out for the phone and tapped in Crisp's mobile number.

'Where are you, lad?'

'In my car, just pulling into the station car park, sir.'

'Come straight up to my office. I've got a job for you.'

A few minutes later, Crisp knocked on the door.

'I want you to pick up Moira Elsworth,' Angel said. 'I asked her to call in so that we could take her fingerprints a few days ago. She never arrived. Also I want to interview her. I don't have her address, but you know where her mother's flower kiosk is, don't you? Start there.'

'Yes. Right, sir.'

'Now look, Trevor, she's a strikingly beautiful young woman. All I want you to do is deliver her here and let me interview her before you start making any romantic advances towards her.'

'I don't chase *every* woman that comes along, sir.'

'If they're under fifty and don't have a face like Red Rum you're after them as if sex was going out of fashion.'

'That's not fair.'

'It might not be fair, but it's true. Now hop off, lad, and bring in Moira Elsworth.'

'Yes, sir,' Crisp said and made for the door, when somebody knocked on it.

'See who it is, lad.'

It was DC Ted Scrivens.

'Come in, Ted,' Angel said.

Crisp and Scrivens acknowledged each other with a nod. Then Crisp went out and closed the door.

Angel said, 'Now then, lad, have you managed to trace the family of that chap Bottomley?'

'Yes, sir. I was glad of that message you sent by Ahmed.'

'Good. Right, lad. Tell me what you got.'

'The young priest at St Cecilia's Church, where Bottomley's funeral service was held, has only been in the job a year, so he didn't know the family. I traced the previous priest and he didn't know them either. There were some records, however. His widow's address at the time of the funeral was given, but she had moved twice since then. I eventually caught up with her, still living in Bromersley. She was living in Canal Street.'

Angel's eyebrows lowered and his face creased. Canal Street was the roughest and lowest street in town. He felt sorry for anyone living down there.

'She denied that she was Bettina Aimee Bottomley at first,' Scrivens said, 'as she had reverted to her maiden name. She was eighty-two years of age and lived with her daughter, Patrice, and her son-in-law. When I mentioned the robbery in 1983 she became quite angry. She said that Ronald had got twelve years for robbing the Royal Westminster Bank in 1983, but that she had not seen a penny of it, also that he had died three years later in a hospital while serving time in Franklin prison, Durham. She said that Vernon Almond had also been found guilty with him and that he had been sent to serve his time in Armley. She had heard that he had died last year. His widow sent her a letter from an address in Leeds. She hadn't heard from her since.'

'You've got the address?'

'Yes, of course, sir.'

'They also had a son, Sean. Did she mention him?'

'No, sir, but I asked her where he was and how he was doing.

And she said that she saw him from time to time and that he was doing very well.'

'Right, lad,' Angel said. 'Great stuff. Did you find out anything else worth knowing?'

'Don't think so, sir.'

'Well, follow up that lead to Vernon Almond's widow in Leeds. Let's see if that produces anything more helpful.'

Scrivens grinned, stood up and said, 'Right, sir,' and went out.

A few minutes later Crisp arrived.

'I've got Moira Elsworth and Gerald Mackenzie in interview room number one, sir,' he said. 'Her mother insisted that she had a solicitor present.'

Angel shrugged. Having a solicitor present meant that he could interview as hard as the solicitor would allow without there being any argument later about who said what, and complaints about bullying and charges that he had taken advantage of her gender and age and all that, so Angel wasn't put out at all. Anyway, every word uttered would be recorded.

'All right, lad. You'd better sit in on this with me, Trevor,' he said, getting up from his desk.

They both made their way out of the office and a short way up the corridor to the brown door marked 'Interview Room 1'.

Having thanked them both for coming in, Angel sat opposite Moira Elsworth, and Crisp opposite Gerald Mackenzie.

Angel switched on the recording machine, checked that he could see both spools rotating, made the usual introductions and then said, 'Miss Elsworth, four days ago, on Tuesday, when I saw you at your mother's shop, I asked you to call here as soon as you could, with Mr Morris, to give us your fingerprints for elimination purposes, but you failed to arrive. Are you prepared to leave your fingerprints with us now?'

'Yes, of course. I am sorry that I have not been sooner, but to tell the truth, Inspector, I forgot all about it.'

Angel wasn't very pleased. His lips tightened back against his teeth. 'Your grandfather had been murdered, and the only thing you could possibly have done to help us find the culprit was to give us your fingerprints for elimination purposes, and you forgot all about it?'

Moira's face went scarlet. She lowered her head.

'In addition,' Angel said, 'I discover that Mr Morris has left his flat in Tunistone in a big hurry. He has disappeared without trace, without leaving a forwarding address, also without leaving us his prints.'

'I'm sorry,' she said.

'An apology is hardly adequate, Miss Elsworth. Perhaps you could tell us why he has disappeared and where he is now?'

'I'm afraid I can't. He said that he had some urgent family business to attend to that wouldn't wait, but that he would be back as soon as he could.'

'And he gave you an address and telephone number where you could get in touch?'

'Well, no, he forgot to say where he was going to – exactly.'

Angel sighed. 'I've heard that song before, Miss Elsworth. I reckon we've seen the last of him.'

'Oh no, Inspector. I'm sure *I* haven't. Look,' she said proudly, holding out her left hand.

On the third finger of the hand was a ring set with a very large single clear stone. She wriggled her fingers slightly to catch the light.

Angel peered at it and blinked. 'Is that a diamond?' he said.

Moira Elsworth withdrew her hand and stared at him indignantly. 'Five point two carats,' she said.

He pursed his lips and shook his head. There was no more

certain a way of fostering and retaining a woman's attention than by putting a big ring on her finger, he thought. If he never returns she will always remember him in a most favourable light.

Angel sighed. 'Have you got a photograph of him?'

'No. That's my only regret,' she said. 'I asked him for one, but he must have forgotten.'

'Would you, by any stretch of the imagination, describe his face as cherubic?'

'Certainly not,' she said. 'There is nothing immature about Charles.'

Angel frowned. She was in love with the man. Hers was a subjective opinion, so he wasn't disposed to query it.

'Do you know anything at all about Charles Morris,' he said, 'that might assist us to find him, anything at all? Did he talk about where he came from or where he intends to go to? Have you any information at all? Please try and remember, it could be extremely important.'

Moira Elsworth shook her pretty little head. 'I'm afraid I haven't a clue. Sorry, Inspector.'

'Did he have an accent … an unusual mannerism? Did he smoke?'

'Did he have a tattoo?' Crisp said.

'Oh no,' she said. 'No. He was … he was perfect.'

'Did he mention his mother, father, brothers, sisters, wives?' Angel said.

Her eyes flashed. 'Certainly not.'

Angel thoughtfully rubbed his chin. He was wondering whether to play his ace or not. Eventually he said, 'Would it surprise you, Miss Elsworth, to learn that his name is not Charles Morris?'

'It certainly would, Inspector,' she said. Then she added, 'What is it, then?'

'The Charles Morris he is pretending to be died last November in Hull.'

'You've obviously got the wrong Charles Morris,' she said. 'I suppose there might be a few people in the country called Charles Morris.'

'There's no mistake on our part, Miss Elsworth, I assure you.'

'What is his real name, then?'

'We don't know. We expected you to tell us.'

Her eyes flashed. 'It's just a trick, isn't it, to get me to betray him?'

'Not at all. We need to speak to him to assist us with our enquiries, that's all. If he's innocent, he's nothing to worry about.'

'Well, I don't believe you.'

Angel blew out a lungful of air. He didn't really believe *her*. He rubbed his chin and said, 'Well, I'm afraid I must warn you that it's an offence to withhold any information that would assist us in our enquiries. You could be fined or even imprisoned.'

Gerald Mackenzie said, 'With respect, Inspector Angel, I don't think it's necessary to threaten Miss Elsworth.'

'I'm not threatening her, Mr Mackenzie, only reminding her of the facts of the situation.'

Moira Elsworth turned back to her solicitor and said, 'He doesn't frighten me with his threats, Mr Mackenzie. He has had the money taken away from us and now my mother has to go to the crown court.'

'That is *stolen* money,' Angel said. 'It doesn't belong to *you* or your mother. Now, if you can't or won't tell me how I can get in touch with Charles Morris—'

'I don't know how to reach him,' she said. 'I wish I did. I *honestly* wish I did, Inspector.'

Angel looked closely at her. Her moist eyes twinkled in the light. Angel wondered if the tears were genuine.

'Right. Thank you,' he said. Then he looked at the recording machine to check that the red light was still on. 'Interview terminated at 15.25 hours.'

Angel reached over to the recorder, switched it off, took the tape out of the machine, and then whispered to Crisp, 'Make sure you get her prints before she leaves the station. Don't take no for an answer. Then come down to my office.'

'Right, sir,' Crisp said and he followed the fragrant Miss Elsworth and her solicitor, Gerald Mackenzie, out of the interview room.

Angel switched off the light, closed the door and returned to his office to find Flora Carter waiting at the door. She was holding several sheets of A4.

He looked at what was in her hand and said, 'Is that the latest copy of Christine Elsworth's accounts, Flora?'

'Yes, sir,' she said brightly.

'Good,' he said, giving her a quick smile. 'Come in, lass,' he said as he pushed open the door and made his way round to his desk. 'Sit down.'

She passed the papers to him.

'Fire away,' he said, taking the papers.

He looked through them as she spoke. 'You'll see that Christine Elsworth does very well. The inspector of taxes pointed out to me that she seems able to sell the flowers at an enormously high margin of profit. There's nothing illegal about that, he said, but it is hardly credible. If she buys six hundred pounds' worth of flowers, she usually sells them for about five times that, say three thousand pounds or more. Whereas, he was saying, the competition spending the same amount might sell them for only twelve hundred pounds. In addition, all flower shops put in a claim for about 10 per cent or 15 per cent wastage, sometimes more. Mrs Elmore doesn't claim for any waste. That suggests that she sells her stock far more quickly than the competition and therefore doesn't incur any waste.'

Angel looked up from the papers. 'I have taken on board all that you have said, Flora, and I agree it is strange. It's not the only thing that's strange. Did the inspector of taxes say anything about her accountant's charges?'

'He said he thought they were rather high.'

'I would say so. She's claiming that she pays King and Company £600 a week. That's over £40,000 a year. From such a small sales outlet that's not realistic, is it?'

'Maybe he does all the bookkeeping, sir? It can be so boring.'

'But it's for a little shop not much bigger than a double prison cell.'

'Oh. I didn't know. I haven't seen the place.' Her forehead creased. 'Is Mr King taking advantage of her, sir?'

'I don't know, Flora,' he said. 'There might be a perfectly reasonable explanation.'

Flora Carter shook her head.

Angel pursed his lips. Then suddenly he put the papers relating to Christine Elsworth's accounts together and pushed them back into her hands. 'Take these—'

The phone rang.

He snatched it up. 'Angel,' he said.

'It's Don Taylor of SOCO, sir. I have a result on—'

'Hold on a minute, Don.'

He turned back to Flora and said, 'Look, Flora, take those accounts. See Christine Elsworth and see what she has to say about it, and let me know the outcome.'

She stood up. 'Right, sir,' she said. She went quickly out of the office and closed the door.

Into the phone Angel said, 'Now then, Don. Sorry about that. You said you had a result?'

Taylor said, 'Yes, sir. That Yogi Bear mask recovered with the money in Christine Elsworth's cellar … it has two persons' prints on it: they are Ernest Piddington's and Christine Elsworth's.'

Angel wrinkled his nose. That was no surprise at all. 'Right,' he said. 'The old man's would be prints from the time he robbed the bank, and his daughter's recently, since she found the money.'

'That sounds right, sir. And the only clear prints on the second Yogi Bear mask found in Morris's rubbish were the same as those found at the back of the wall clock in his flat. We've emailed them to Records, sir, and they've come back "Not identified".'

Angel rubbed his chin. 'It might be that Morris – or whatever his name is – has not yet been caught, so Records wouldn't have his dabs on file.'

'Could be,' Taylor said.

There was a knock on the door.

'Come in,' Angel called, then into the phone he said, 'Anything else, Don?'

'No, sir, that's all I've got,' Taylor said.

Angel replaced the phone.

It was Crisp at the door. Angel saw that he was holding a fingerprint card by its edges. He smiled. 'Ah! You got them, lad? Good.'

'Still wet, sir.'

'Right, well let Don Taylor have them. He has some important comparisons to make.'

'Right, sir,' Crisp said. 'By the way, sir, there's been no change in the matter of the white van.'

Angel frowned. 'What white van?'

'You remember my telling you about a white van parked outside Gregg's newsagent's shop?'

'Oh yes. What about it? It isn't a restricted area, so the driver can park his van there for as long as he likes. It has a valid road tax disc. It isn't a derelict. It hasn't got bald tyres or anything, has it? He isn't breaking any laws, is he?'

'No, sir. It's not that the driver is doing anything illegal. It's just a bit strange that even though the van is parked there for hours and hours, old man Gregg never can catch the driver. It's driven away late at night, and it appears back on that parking space around lunchtime the next day. Mr Gregg mentioned it again to me when I went in for a paper this morning. It is really annoying him. He reckons it is keeping some of his customers away.'

Angel waved his arm and said, 'Well, I'm sorry if his sales of the *Beano* are down, lad ... I wish that's all I had to worry about.'

The phone rang. He reached out for it. 'Angel,' he said.

There was a loud coughing in his ear. He recognized the initiator of the cough as Superintendent Harker. The racket persisted for another ten seconds, then it stopped and the superintendent said, 'Ah yes, Angel, I want you up here ASAP.' The phone was then slammed down.

Angel frowned as he replaced the handset. He looked at Crisp. 'I'm wanted in the super's office.' He pointed to the print card Crisp was still holding. 'Get those prints down to Don Taylor before you smudge them.'

'Right, sir,' Crisp said and then he made for the door.

Angel was right behind him out of the office. Crisp went down the corridor, and Angel went up.

FOURTEEN

Angel knocked on Harker's door, pushed it open and went inside. The usual Mediterranean heat and smell of menthol hit him as soon as he turned to close the door.

Harker, partly hidden by several piles of ledgers, papers and files on his desk, said, 'Ah, there you are, lad. Been waiting for you.'

Angel's face creased. 'I came straightaway, sir.'

'Don't argue, lad. Sit down and we can begin.'

He noticed that DI Asquith was present and sitting facing the super's desk.

Asquith looked across at him, nodded in acknowledgement, and pointed to the chair next to him.

Angel sat down.

Harker cleared his throat noisily, then said, 'Now, I've asked you both here again to give you the opportunity to report on what I said to you last Tuesday ... about gangs. I asked you then if either of you had any notion of a gang of, say, four or more crooks, working together on our patch. I have heard nothing from either of you and the Chief Constable needs to know what you have to say.'

Angel looked at Asquith, who didn't seem to have anything to say.

'Well, sir,' Angel said. 'I have nothing to report. I understand that the Chief has the facility to call in an external unit to overcome such a situation, but I am not aware of any gang functioning on our patch at the moment.' He then turned to look at Haydn Asquith.

'I am not aware of any gangs either, sir,' Asquith said. 'We occasionally get a disturbance created by kids up on Nelson Mandela Gardens, which you already know about. But they are kids and we can easily contain it.'

Harker looked as if he had just smelled the drains at Armley. 'I am not talking about juveniles,' he said. 'I am talking about gangs of evil men who manoeuvre themselves into positions where they can put the screws on senior policemen, bank officials, judges, politicians or anyone else in a position of power over others, or have control over huge sums of cash or valuables. Those are the sort of evil monsters we are looking for.'

Angel and Asquith looked up at him. Angel noticed that the superintendent's head looked like a skull with ears stuck on.

Harker looked from one to the other and back. 'Well, is that it, then?' he said. 'Have neither of you anything to contribute? The Chief feels that he should put *something* in his report.'

Angel couldn't think of anything else useful to say. He just looked at him.

Asquith also remained silent.

Harker waited a few more seconds, then he sighed, sniffed and said, 'Right. Carry on, DI Asquith. Hold fast, DI Angel. I have something else I want to say to you.'

Angel's heart dropped down to his boots. He couldn't think what the superintendent wanted. Harker could see how the case was going from Angel's daily reports.

Asquith nodded at Harker, then Angel, and said, 'Right, sir,' and went out.

When the door was closed, Harker peered across at Angel and said, 'I see that you have let your prime suspect, Charles Morris, slip through your fingers?'

Angel shuffled a little in the chair. It was true. It was difficult to defend it. 'I am not sure he is my prime suspect, sir,' he said. 'He is one of several.'

'You realize that if he commits another murder before he is caught, there would have to be an inquiry into your professionalism in the matter?'

Angel felt his heart begin to pound at the thought of the suggestion that he could be responsible for anybody's death. And he certainly didn't want an inquiry into his method of working, which had not failed to let him down in the past. He didn't want to be hidebound by a system called HOLMES 2, which was an acronym for a Home Office Large Major Enquiry System, and had nothing to do with the great fictional character, Sherlock Holmes. HOLMES 2 was a methodical and overwhelmingly detailed and laborious (thus expensive) system currently used in the investigation of murder and other big crimes by the larger police forces.

'I hope my methods will be seen to be satisfactory, sir,' he said.

Harker wrinkled his nose and said, 'I see. You're hoping that your record will hold you in good stead. You flatter yourself. I tell you, Angel, another death at the hands of Charles Morris would not be justified. You failed to arrest him when you had the opportunity, and you cannot get away from the fact.'

Angel was momentarily stuck for words. In essence what Harker said was true, but there were extenuating circumstances.

'I don't see how I could possibly be held responsible for someone's death at the hands of Charles Morris,' Angel said. 'He disappeared before I had sufficient evidence to arrest him.'

'Aah,' Harker said. 'That's exactly the fine point a judge and jury would have to decide.'

Angel's facial muscles tightened and his fingers gripped the ends of the chair arms.

Harker looked at him. He concealed a smirk. Eventually he

said, 'Well, let's hope it doesn't come to that.' His thin eyebrows arched upwards. 'Now, you said you had other suspects. Who are they?'

'Well, it's early days, but I am not happy about Christine Elsworth for one.'

Harker's eyebrows arched up even higher. 'A woman murdering her own father? Sounds a bit far-fetched. Tell me the others.'

Angel wished he had had time to get ready for this. Harker was catching him grossly unprepared.

'There are others chasing the stash of money that had been hidden in Piddington's attic. Before each of the men died they would naturally but quite wrongly have told their families that they were entitled to a share of the money held for them by Ernest Piddington and the families may have had to murder old man Piddington, trying to find out where it was hidden.'

'Maybe. Maybe. What are their names, and, if that were so, why was Nancy Quinn murdered?'

'It could have been because she had discovered the hiding place, told her boyfriend—'

'Charles Morris?'

' – then he murdered her to keep the money for himself.'

Harker frowned. 'Well, why didn't he take the money before he disappeared, then?'

'I don't know, sir.'

'Hmmm. And I thought Morris was involved with Moira Elsworth.'

'He was, but it wouldn't have stopped him having a relationship with Nancy Quinn at the same time.'

He nodded, then said, 'You haven't told me who your other suspects are.'

'Anybody who was related to any of the three robbers, Almond, Bottomley and Piddington, sir. Almond had one son, Bottomley had a son and a daughter, and Piddington had a daughter and a grown-up granddaughter.'

'What about the spouses?'

'Scrivens is looking up Almond's widow as we speak. Bottomley's widow is eighty-two and in poor circumstances, and Piddington's widow has passed on.'

'That makes six or seven suspects, lad,' Harker said. 'Well, I'd better let you crack on and try and solve these two murders,' he said, then he added with a sneer, 'in your usual idiosyncratic way. But you'll have to get a move on. Time is money, you know.'

Angel wasn't pleased.

Angel returned to his office and sat down at his desk. He could have committed a murder himself, but he soon recovered and began to think constructively about all the loose ends connected with the two murders he had to solve and was happy that every line of inquiry was being properly investigated. He was awaiting several important pieces of forensic information from Dr Mac and the laboratory at Wetherby, but he knew that the processes of science take time. The murders were only committed five days ago so he would have to be patient for a few more.

His mind went back to Harker's question about the presence of gangs in Bromersley. He could not think of any at the moment. He remembered in the early nineties, there had been a gang of crooked moneylenders who were terrorizing householders on their doorsteps and in their homes, but they had managed to stamp that out. His mind wandered back to what Crisp had been saying about the white van parked outside Gregg's the newsagent's. The driver was entitled to park in that little square as long as he wanted. Perhaps the driver lived nearby. The van had been parking there every day for about two weeks. Strange that Gregg didn't challenge the driver and ask him to move. Crisp said that Gregg never saw the driver. It was as if there wasn't one. There had to be a driver. According to Crisp, the van was moved late at night and returned late the following morning. It always parked on the same space.

Angel heard the church clock strike five. Home time, and a weekend to look forward to. He gathered all the post, papers and files not dealt with onto one heap and stuffed it into a desk drawer. Then he reached out for his coat, switched out the light and closed the door.

He was home in fifteen minutes. He let himself in by the kitchen door as Mary was peering into the oven.

'You're home early, darling,' she said. 'Everything all right?'

'I'm not really early,' he said, giving her a kiss.

It was the time he would always arrive home if he didn't get carried away with the job and forget, or was delayed by circumstances. He crossed the kitchen to the fridge and took out a can of German beer.

Mary watched him and passed him a tumbler from the draining board.

He smiled in acknowledgement.

Then she said, 'I don't suppose you know where the Peterloo massacre occurred?'

'I've heard of it,' Angel said with a frown. Then he said, 'Whatever do you want to know that for? Is it one of those daft magazine quizzes again?'

'They're not daft. You can win really good prizes if you can get all the answers right. It was somewhere in Russia, wasn't it?'

'It was Manchester ... early in the 1800s, I think. And if you're chosen out of thousands and thousands of entries. Of course you've a much better chance if you're the daughter of the chairman of the publisher of the magazine.' He had a sip of the beer. It tasted good. He held it up to the light.

'Manchester?' she said.

'It was a political thing … a dreadful incident. Some people murdered and many wounded with sabres. Peterloo was a made-up word. Something to do with combining the name of the place in Manchester where the massacre took place, St Peter's Field, with the Battle of Waterloo that had taken place only a year or two earlier.'

She went into the sitting room, wrote the answer in the magazine, came back into the kitchen, looked at him and said, 'Know-all.'

He smiled and took another sip of the beer. 'What's for tea?' he said.

'Salmon. Would you like to set the table?'

After tea, Angel went into the sitting room with Mary. They were enjoying their coffee and watching the news on television. The world and national news was followed by the local news, which was mostly a preview of the National Jewellery Fair to the trade, opening in Leeds on Tuesday next. There were interviews with the chairman of the fair followed by several jewellers who had interesting, rare gemstones set in silver, gold or platinum that would be on display and offered for sale to the trade at the fair. An interview that was of particular interest to Angel was with Lady Tulliver from Tunistone. She said that her husband was going to open the trade fair next Tuesday morning and that she would be with him wearing the famous Mermaid Diamond pendant. She was asked to explain how the stone became known as the Mermaid Diamond and to retell its origins, which she did most delightfully. The announcer then introduced the weatherman and there the news programme ended.

Angel knew that the stone was worth a seven-figure sum and would be the target of every lowlife thief in the business. While the

39-carat stone was too well known to be sold as it was, it could be cut by an expert jeweller into several smaller stones and sold piecemeal. Although this would very much reduce the value, it would still produce a substantial sum, well worth the effort of a gang of dedicated thieves.

The more Angel thought about the Mermaid Diamond, the more he thought it would be stolen. Such a supposition was hard for him to dismiss, and he considered that the interview with Lady Tulliver was tantamount to a challenge to all thieves.

Unfortunately, it was one of those rainy weekends when it never seemed to stop. There was nothing of interest on the television and he had read all his library books. Finding nothing to distract him over the two days, his mind toyed with ways and means of stealing the big stone. It became an entertainment for him ... devising plans how he would set about stealing the diamond without being caught, if he were a thief.

By the time Monday morning arrived, in his imagination he had stolen the valuable stone and got away with it four times.

FIFTEEN

It was 8.28 a.m. when Angel made his way down the corridor to his office. As he took off his coat and hung it on the hook on the side of the stationery cupboard, there was a knock at the door. 'Come in,' Angel called.

It was DC Scrivens. 'I couldn't see Mrs Almond on Friday afternoon, sir. When I got there the house was locked up both back and front. I knocked and knocked, but there was nobody in.'

'Did you look through the windows?'

'Everything looked all right, sir. All neat and tidy. All windows closed. So I asked a neighbour, but she didn't know anything.'

The phone rang. He reached out for it. 'Yes, Angel.'

'DS Clifton. Duty sergeant, sir. Good morning.'

'Good morning, Bernie. What is this … so early in the day?'

'It's late in the day for me, sir. I have a man in the reception waiting room anxiously wanting to see you. He wouldn't explain to anybody what he wanted except that he had a crime to report and he wanted to report it to you.'

Angel wrinkled his nose, blew out a foot of air, then said, 'What's his name?'

'Vittorio Ramazzotti. Do you know him?'

Angel blinked. 'Never heard of him. Did he say it was urgent?'

'He did, sir. He's been waiting more than an hour.'

'Right, Bernie, thank you,' he said, resigned to hearing what Vittorio Ramazzotti wanted to tell him. 'I'll send Ahmed up to collect him in a couple of minutes.'

Angel returned the phone to its holster and turned back to Scrivens. 'I'd better come with you to Leeds. Yes. I have a man waiting to see me; when he's gone, we'll go in my car. All right?'

Scrivens looked relieved. 'Yes, sir. I'll wait in the CID room, sir.'

'Will you ask Ahmed to bring Mr Vittorio Ramazzotti to me? He's in the reception waiting room.'

'Of course, sir,' he said and he went out.

Three minutes later there was a knock on Angel's office door. 'Come in.'

It was Ahmed.

'Mr Vittorio Ramazzotti, sir,' Ahmed said as he showed the small man with the Van Dyke beard into Angel's office.

Angel said, 'Thank you, Ahmed.'

Ramazzotti also turned round to thank Ahmed, but he had gone and the door was closed.

'Ah, Inspector Angel,' Ramazzotti said. 'There you are. I recognize you from your photograph. It is my very great pleasure to meet you, I am sure.'

He reached out for Angel's hand, held it tight and shook it, pumping it up and down without letting go, until Angel managed to pull it away.

Ramazzotti realized what he had done and a little embarrassed said, '*Scusi*.' He moved his hands and arms around excitedly as he spoke.

Angel smiled. 'That's all right. Please sit down, Mr Ramazzotti, and tell me the nature of the crime you have to report.'

'Of course. And thank you. May I say what a great honour it is to have you listen to my story which is a great mystery to me.'

'What is the nature of the crime exactly?'

'It is a mystery, Inspector Angel, a mystery that has confounded me these past few days.'

'But has a crime been committed, Mr Ramazzotti? You are here to report an incident where someone has broken the law, aren't you?'

'Yes. Oh yes, indeed. I have longed to meet you since I first read about you in the *Canadian Picture Pictorial*, where you have taken the motto of the Mounties, that you always get your man.'

Angel sighed. 'You live in Bromersley, do you, Mr Ramazzotti?'

'Indeed I do, Inspector. I live in Clement Attlee Square. I ran a musical instrument shop there. Unfortunately the good people of Bromersley are not interested in the making of their own music. They prefer to listen to others on the discs making millions. So I could not sell the instruments any more. I went into the discs and sold some, but now they take them for free from the World Wide Web at no charge, so I cannot make a profit from selling discs. Alas, I say to myself, what shall I do, when I see in the newspaper this advertisement.'

He took out a small newspaper cutting from a battered leather wallet and passed it over to Angel. 'Please to read it, Inspector. Your reading of the English is much better than mine.'

Angel took it. It was a small ad in the personal column of the *Bromersley Chronicle*. He noted that the date of the ad was Friday, 19 April 2013. He read it silently.

It said:

Golden Opportunity with *The International String Music Foundation*!

Wanted: a suitably experienced double-bass player for part-time employment. Bursary of £700 per week offered.

A representative of *The International String Music Foundation* will be at the Feathers Hotel, Bromersley, between noon and 5 p.m. on Saturday, 20 April 2013 to interview. Candidate must be accomplished, have flair and be able to work on his or her own. Great opportunity for suitably qualified musician. Apply in person.

Angel rubbed his chin, read the ad again and then put the cutting on his desk under the telephone holster.

'Now, Inspector,' Ramazzotti said, 'I play ze bass fiddle. I learn it as a boy in Milano. I played it professionally in Italy, and I have played in professional orchestras in Sheffield and amateur orchestras in and around Bromersley for years. I have lately played for Gilbert and Sullivan societies' productions of *Iolanthe*, *Pirates of Penzance*, *The Mikado*, as well as light operas such as *Die Fledermaus*, and so on.'

Angel brushed his hand through his hair, leaned forward over his desk and said, 'Yes, Mr Ramazzotti, but what offence has been committed?'

'I am coming to that, Inspector. Please to listen to me. *Uno minuto*, if you pleeese! Well, where was I? Ah yes. I went to the Feathers Hotel, I sat in a room set aside as a waiting room for two hours. There were six other candidates. Some looked very young. I didn't believe I would get the job. I was eventually interviewed by a director of *The International String Music Foundation*.

'I was told that the big man ... the chairman of *The International String Music Foundation* had been a keen double-bass player and was also keen on the works of Gilbert and Sullivan. As a surprise, the committee had decided to engage a double-bass player who has the necessary flair and ability to transpose the music of Sir Arthur Sullivan so that the double bass played a more significant part in the music throughout.

'The man also said that if my work was satisfactory, it would be published and performed in the West End and then, possibly,

New York. He asked me a few questions and then asked me to play my double bass. He seemed satisfied with all that and put me on his shortlist of three. Then he told me the conditions of the employment. I have them here somewhere.'

Ramazzotti began fumbling around in his inside pocket. At length he produced a folded sheet of A4 and unfolded it carefully.

Angel sighed. 'I suppose you are going to tell me the conditions,' he said.

'*Sì*, Inspector Angel. It is necessary for you to understand the crime,' he said.

'Oh, there *is* a crime?' Angel said.

'The conditions,' Ramazzotti said. 'I wrote them down on this paper so that there would be no misunderstanding. I read. "(1) All writing and rehearsing must be done in premises appropriate to keep the work secret, also to avoid any possible annoyance to neighbours. Such premises to be determined and approved by *The International String Music Foundation*,

(2) Applicants must be prepared to work each evening from five o'clock to midnight, seven days a week until the work is finished, and

(3) A bursary of £700 per week to be paid by our representative at the end of each week."'

Ramazzotti then folded the paper and put it back into his pocket.

'I said that I would agree to all those conditions and would be glad to be given the opportunity. He asked me to wait. Three of us waited. I waited another half an hour, then he called me in and offered me the job. Oh, I was so pleased, Inspector! To get the job against thirty-six other people, all, I believe, younger than I.'

Angel looked at the clock on the wall, shook his head and wondered if he could suggest to Ramazzotti that he came back tomorrow to finish the story, but the little man did sound as if he was reaching the conclusion.

'So I started the job on 25 April. It was necessary to travel to Tunistone to work. I worked as arranged beginning with *The Mikado*. At 5 p.m. on the 2 May, the man from *The International String Music Foundation* looked at the manuscript I had written. He said that it looked excellent and I was duly paid the £700 in cash. I continued working as they wanted, but last Thursday, 9 May, again, when I was due for a second visit at Tunistone from him and payment of £700, nobody came. I continued to turn up for work on the Friday, Saturday and yesterday, but still no sign of the Foundation man. I am still working hard, but he does not come. They now owe me over a thousand pounds. They seem to have vanished into thin air. There is the mystery, Inspector Angel, and *there* is the crime.'

Angel frowned and rubbed his chin. It certainly was a strange story, but he was not certain that he could find any criminal act there. Even if Mr Ramazzotti had not received payment for work done, it might not be a matter for the police. It was possibly a labour dispute.

'Mr Ramazzotti, are you a member of a trade union?'

'You mean like the Musicians' Union? I used to be, but no. I am not. Should I be?'

Angel blew out a length of air. 'Never mind,' he said. 'I will look into it, when I can. Firstly, I will need to know the address of the Foundation.'

'I'm afraid I haven't got that, Inspector.'

'Didn't you have a letter or a card or something, the conditions of employment you spoke of?'

'I'm afraid not. You understand, Inspector, I wanted the job. I didn't want to be … erm to be … er difficult. I take everything from what he say, not what he didn't write down.'

Angel blinked. 'Well, all right,' he said. 'What were the names and addresses of the men who interviewed you, engaged you and subsequently paid you?'

'They were all the same man, Inspector. I just called him "sir".'

'Well, what did he look like?'

'He look just like my older brother, Emilio,' he said with a big smile.

Angel's jaw muscles tightened. 'Have you a photograph of Emilio?'

'No. He lives in Milano with my dear mother. Some time ago, he went to a seminary in Rome, to study to be a priest, but he met a young woman and she led him away from his vocation. I do not know where he is. I haven't seen him for eight years now. My mother is distraught.'

Angel ran his hand through his hair. 'She's not the only one,' he thought. He shook his head, then said, 'All right, Mr Ramazzotti, do you know the address of the place in Tunistone where you worked?'

'Of course. It was St Cuthbert's parish hall on Church Street.'

'Ah! And who did you see or meet while you were there writing and playing?'

'Nobody. It was a lonely existence. The door was always unlocked for me when I arrived at five o'clock, and I was to put out the lights, drop the latch and close the door when I left at midnight.'

Angel's face muscles tightened. He wiped his hand impatiently across his face.

It was ten minutes later that the little Italian left Angel's office, much to Angel's relief. Angel promptly opened a file and labelled it 'Double bass/Vittorio Ramazzotti' and dropped his notes into it, hoping that the mysterious and unusual story would have a logical, happy and glorious ending without needing any effort on his part.

However, the remarkable story told him by the double-bass-

playing Italian was to dominate his subconscious and preoc-
cupy him when his mind was not involved in matters
immediately all-consuming until the mystery was completely
solved. His mind – more than most other people's – worked in
an unfathomable way. He did not have complete control over it,
and it was easily sidetracked by what he saw, heard, smelled or
remembered.

He pulled open the top drawer of the filing cabinet and was
placing the new file between 'Dangerous substances' and
'Emergency call-out' when the phone rang. It was Don Taylor.

'I thought you'd like to know, sir, that the prints on the back of
old Mr Piddington's wheelchair are not those of Moira Elsworth.'

Angel frowned. 'Thank you, Don,' he said. He banged down the
phone. He was not pleased. He pursed his lips. It was not Moira
Elsworth.

But who could be the one who dragged that wheelchair with a
92-year-old grandfather in it to the top of the staircase and then
simply let it go, watching him and the chair drop down the steps,
throwing the old man out, who then rolled over and over and
came to rest at the bottom on the parquet floor with a broken
neck.

He was still weighing the probabilities when there was a knock
at the door.

It was Flora Carter.

'Come in, lass,' he said and pointed to the chair. 'You've seen
Christine Elsworth?'

'Yes, sir,' Flora said. 'I told her that we had seen last year's
accounts which she had submitted to HMRC and that we were
surprised to see that she had paid a total of £31,200 to King and
Company for his accounting services for the year 2012/13.'

'She was quick to say that he was very good with his advice to
her.'

'He needed to be. Did you ask her how she managed to earn such huge profits – over 300 per cent – when other similar florists only manage around 50 per cent?'

'Yes, sir. She had no real answer other than that she worked very hard and kept long hours.'

'That really won't do, Flora. It isn't realistic … such profits from a tiny shop. It simply isn't good enough. I've been thinking about this. This is what I think was happening. Christine Elsworth was regularly introducing stolen money from her father's loft into her cash till at the kiosk. Whenever anybody bought flowers and required change, she gave it to them in the old stolen notes and retained the legitimate notes. Also, when she paid her suppliers, she paid them with stolen notes. But when she banked her takings, she paid in only legitimate notes. Christine Elsworth worked hard at buying good flowers and selling as many as she could at competitive prices, but it really didn't matter how profitable or unprofitable the flower kiosk was because it was merely a front for laundering money big-time. And Andrew King of King and Company, her accountant, must have been complicit in the fiddle. He was, possibly, the brains behind it, and he was supposed to have covered it up in the accounts. So get a warrant to seize Christine Elsworth's cash till and check it for any stolen notes, also her handbag. Of course, she may not have any of the stolen notes any more because the bulk of the money has now been handed over to the court, but she's a sly old fox, she has probably got some stuffed down her stocking leg or hidden in the fridge or somewhere. You'll have to move quickly.'

She nodded. 'What about Andrew King, sir?'

Angel rubbed his chin thoughtfully. His face hardened. 'You can bet he's fireproof, but charge him, and collate as much information as you can and let us hope that Mr Twelvetrees at the CPS can make a case against him stick.'

'Right, sir,' she said, getting to her feet, then she looked at him closely. 'Christine Elsworth's going to *love* you,' she said.

He shrugged, then pursed his lips. 'Huh. That's a burden I will have to bear, Flora,' he said lightly. 'Now you'd better shift. You'll need some help. Take two PCs with you.'

'Yes. Right, sir,' she said and she was gone.

Angel looked up at the clock. It was eleven o'clock already. He remembered his arrangement with Scrivens. He reached over for his coat and pushed an arm into a sleeve, then put on his hat and rushed out of the office. He crossed the corridor to the CID office, stuck his head in, saw Ahmed and Scrivens talking to each other. Both men saw him and stood up.

Angel looked at Scrivens. 'Come on, lad.' Then he turned to Ahmed. 'I'm going to Leeds, if you want me, you can get me on my mobile.'

'Right, sir,' Ahmed said.

Angel and Scrivens made their way quickly down the corridor, past the cells and through the back door to the car park and the BMW. Angel drove and Scrivens navigated. Forty-five minutes later they were in the middle of a large Victorian estate of terraced houses on the northern side of Leeds.

Angel thought the streets were unusually quiet for the time of day. He saw a woman washing the outside of the windows of an upstairs room by sitting outside on the window ledge with her legs and feet dangling inside the bedroom. Two boys aged about ten were kicking a tin can ahead of them in turns as they ran along the pavement.

Angel stopped the BMW outside the front door of number 166 Sebastopol Terrace. The two men got out of the car.

Angel said, 'You take the back, Ted, I'll do the front. I'll give you five seconds. And have a peek through the window.'

'Right, sir,' Scrivens said and he moved quickly through a narrow ginnel in the row, which led to the back doors.

Angel peered through the net curtains into number 166, but could see only a sideboard loaded with pot ornaments and, nearer, the arm of a sofa. No signs of life.

He waited a few moments, then knocked on the door. There was no reply. He knocked again, more urgently.

Suddenly, the front door of the house next door opened, and a woman wearing a yellow cloth in the form of a turban and a flowered overall came out, stood on the doorstep and leaned against the door jamb. She looked Angel up and down, then took a cigarette end out of her pocket, lit it, took a big drag, blew out a cloud of smoke and folded her arms.

Eventually she said, 'Looking for Bettina Almond?'

Angel looked back at her and smiled. 'Yes, I am actually.'

'Are you from the police?'

'Yes,' he said. 'Is Mrs Almond out?'

'What's she been up to?'

Angel blinked. 'What time will she back?'

'Couldn't say,' she said, taking another drag on the cigarette end.

Angel nodded. 'Right. Thank you very much.' He frowned. He was thinking of going round to the back door to contact Scrivens. It looked like a wasted journey. He couldn't afford the time to hang around.

The woman suddenly said, 'She'll not be back today. She's in hospital ... the LGI. Going to have an operation. Taken sudden.' Then she rolled her eyes, pointed downwards and silently mouthed the words, 'Down below ... all to be taken away.' This was followed by a single, heavy, knowing nod of the head.

Angel hesitated, then said, 'Er, right. Thank you.'

He went down the ginnel and collected Scrivens. He told him what he had found out and they immediately made their way back to Leeds city centre onto Calverley Street and through the entrance to the car park of Leeds General Infirmary. The lady on the reception desk advised that Mrs Bettina Almond was in a ward in the Jubilee Wing. They made their way along several corridors, up in a lift and the ward they were looking for was facing the lift doors. The Sister in charge was at a desk in a small anteroom busy with several nurses, looking at patients' charts. She looked up.

Angel showed his ID and explained that he needed to see Mrs Almond urgently on police business.

Sister said, 'Well, it is not visiting time, but you can see her for five minutes only. She is in the bed nearest the door.'

'Thank you, Sister,' Angel said. 'I don't think it will take us that long.'

The two policemen made their way to the double swing-doors. Angel reached out for a door handle and pulled it. He stopped when he saw the back of a man in a brown overcoat leaning over the bed nearest to them. Angel allowed the door to close, then he pulled the handle so that there was a half-inch gap between the two doors and he peered through it. The man was in his forties, suntanned and had dark hair. Angel didn't recognize him.

The man was leaning over somebody in a bed. Angel could hear him.

'I'd better go,' the man said. 'I shouldn't be here. Don't worry. Everything will be all right. See you tomorrow afternoon. You will be awake by then.' He leaned down, Angel thought it was to kiss her, then the man turned towards the door.

Angel backed off quickly, pushing Scrivens into the door jamb. 'Sorry, lad.' Angel spat out the following rapidly: 'He's coming out. I'll collar him. You interview the woman. All right?'

Scrivens's mouth dropped open. 'Er – yes. Right, sir.'

The swing door opened. Scrivens went into the ward as the man came out.

Angel stepped in front of the man in the brown overcoat. 'Excuse me, sir. I am a police officer, I wonder if I might have a word with you.'

The man stopped, looked round, then attempted to brush past Angel and make a quick dash along the corridor.

Angel reached out and grabbed him securely by the wrist. 'There's no need to try to run off, sir.'

A look of fear showed in the man's eyes and lips.

Angel also noticed that the man was about the same height as he was, so that he would readily fall into the category of tall, and he was certainly dark and handsome. The two witnesses who saw the murderer also described him as having a cherubic face. Angel wouldn't have described him as having a cherubic face.

The man in the brown overcoat developed a smile. 'I'm so sorry,' he said. 'I don't know why I did that. Did you say you were a police officer?'

'Yes, sir. Just a few questions, to help with our enquiries.'

'What do you want?' the man said.

He looked into Angel's eyes, then down at the iron grip he had round his wrist, then back up to his eyes again. His jaw muscles tightened. 'Do you mind?' he said.

Angel slowly released his grip, watching the man very carefully.

'Thank you,' the man said.

Angel said, 'Have you any means of identification, sir?'

'Whatever for?' the man said as he reached into his inside pocket and took out a wallet. 'What do you want? Bank card, store card, driver's licence ...'

'Driver's licence would be fine.'

The man handed it to him.

Angel read out the name. 'Charles Almond?' He compared the photograph. It was a fair enough likeness. He handed the card back. 'What is your father's first name, Mr Almond?'

'He had two. They were Vernon Alan, and my mother's names are Bettina Aimee. Is there anything else? Is that all you wanted me for? I have matters to attend to.'

'There are a few more questions I have to ask. We need somewhere quiet where we can talk.'

'What's this all about? I was just visiting my mother, she's having a serious operation later today.'

'Yes. Sorry to hear that, sir. But—'

Angel broke off. Over Charles Almond's shoulder, he saw the lift arrive, the doors opened and an attractive young woman stepped out. She looked round. She seemed lost.

Angel's eyes grew bigger. He knew he recognized her. It was Moira Elsworth.

Almond turned round to see what had caught Angel's attention.

Moira had seen him, she smiled and was advancing towards him. He stepped towards her, holding out his arms and they embraced.

'Oh Charles,' she said breathily. 'I'm sorry I'm late. The traffic was dreadful.'

'Darling. Glad you made it,' Almond said.

She put her arm under his and clenched his hand, then she turned and saw Angel. She blinked several times.

'Oh. Excuse me, Inspector, what a coincidence meeting you here. Have you met Inspector Angel, Charles? He's looking into the death of Granddad, you know. This is my boyfriend, Charles Morris.'

'Charles Morris?' Angel said. 'He said his name was Charles Almond.'

SIXTEEN

Mary brought the coffee into the sitting room and put the tray on the table between them.

'Thank you, darling,' Angel said, sitting down in his usual chair. 'Lovely dinner,' he added. 'I like your cottage pie ... I think I've eaten too much.'

She smiled and passed over the coffee cup.

'Anyway, where was I?'

'You were telling me that very curious story about that Italian double-bass player and the—'

'No. I'd finished that, love, although it is still very much on my mind. Do you know, I might nip out for a breath of fresh air, and have a look at his old shop. It's not far. It's in Clement Attlee Square.'

'You'll finish your coffee?'

'Oh yes,' he said, taking a sip.

They sat there in silence for a while, then he said, 'Ah yes, I remember. I was saying that Charles Almond has a satisfactory alibi for the Sunday evening and night of 5 May, the times when Ernest Piddington and Nancy Quinn were murdered; besides that, Almond hasn't a cherubic face, so he isn't the murderer.'

'What about him stealing the identity of Charles Morris? Why did he do that?'

'He admits that he came to Bromersley as Charles Morris originally so that he could get close to Ernest Piddington and the money, without arousing the old man's or the Elsworth's suspicions. Almond's father, of course, before he died had told him all about the robbery in 1983, and that he was entitled to a third of the proceeds which were in the care of Ernest Piddington.'

'Does Moira Elsworth know all this?'

'Almond says he's told her everything.'

'And do you believe him?'

'Well … I suppose I do. But it doesn't matter whether I do or I don't, really, he's got a rock-solid alibi. And he told me that since the court got custody of the money, he has lost interest. He could see that there was no hope of his ever laying his hands on it. Admitting that demonstrates that he is speaking the truth, doesn't it?'

She didn't answer the question; instead she said, 'He's still interested in Moira.'

'Very much. Yes, but *she's* doing most of the chasing. They're a good-looking couple. Lust at first sight and all that … sort of thing.'

Mary smiled, then she said, 'If he thought so much about Moira, why did he leave Tunistone so abruptly?'

'His mother was seriously ill and needed an operation urgently. The news also coincided with the court order to take possession of the stolen money. So his plan was utterly thwarted.'

'But love wins through and he must have contacted Moira after a few days.'

'Exactly.'

'Will he be prosecuted for taking the ID of the real Charles Morris, the man who had died in Hull?'

'I'll have to put it in my report, but I'm not much interested in taking that any further. There's enough to do. However, the super might insist on it.'

Mary sipped the coffee, then said, 'You didn't actually see Mrs Almond?'

'I didn't, no. Ted Scrivens interviewed her. She had nothing to say in the way of usable evidence so I didn't see the need, coupled with the fact that she was not very well. Ted said that she had quite a lot to say about Ernest Piddington. She was indignant that her husband had served eight years in prison and Piddington had got away scot-free. Even so, she trusted him enough for him to hold on to her husband's share until they agreed to divide it. She said that Vernon had told her that the three men had made an agreement that they would not touch the money for at least five years. They looked on it as their pensions. It was actually a lot longer than five years, and now that Mrs Almond could do with a handout, the court has taken possession of it. You can understand her not being pleased with the old man.'

She nodded, then said, 'Having eliminated him, what do you know about the murderer or murderers now?'

Angel breathed out heavily. 'Now that it has been determined that the fingerprints on the back of the wheelchair do not belong to Moira Elsworth, I believe that both murders were committed by this Edward Oliver.'

Mary nodded. 'Are you any nearer finding out who exactly this Edward Oliver is?'

'No. He knows me, so I must know him. He has an educated but menacing voice. He is the conventional tall, dark and handsome character ... and has a cherubic face. The dreadful state of Nancy Quinn's body indicated that he was brutal, cruel and highly sexed. He is probably psychotic. The awful thing is that I must have spoken to him frequently.'

'Well, who is it, then?'

'The damned annoying thing is that I can't place him. I have racked my brain but I can't ...'

'He doesn't sound like a man *I'd* like to come up against,' Mary said.

'I hope you never do, darling. I hope you never do,' he said. He reached out for his coffee and finished it off.

'You must be very careful. He sounds like a very bad lot.'

'I'm always careful.'

'More coffee, sweetheart?' Mary said.

'Please,' he said, passing his cup.

Mary filled the cup, then refilled her own.

'Now, haven't we had enough of this dreary shop talk?' he said. 'Is there anything on the telly?'

'I'll have a look,' she said. She began sorting through the small jumble of magazines and newspapers on the shelf of the library table, looking for the *Radio Times*. She suddenly spotted a magazine with the page open and turned back. 'Oh, by the way, darling, can you help me with this? You might know the answer.' She glanced at the open page and found the place she wanted. She read, '"In what ocean is Easter Island?"'

Angel screwed up his face. 'Is this one of your tatty quiz jobs?'

'They're not tatty … if you don't *know*, say so.'

'It's in the South Pacific somewhere.'

'If you don't know, don't guess.'

'I'm not guessing … don't know exactly where it is. I know it was named Easter Island because it was discovered on Easter Day. And it's in the South Pacific.'

'I'm putting that in. I hope it's right.'

'It is right. Is there any post?'

'Oh yes. I forgot. There's a circular on the sideboard at the end, where I always put it.'

Angel growled and got to his feet. 'Oh yes. It's *always* there, except when it *isn't*. Sometimes you shove it in my hand, or put in front of me at the table, or it's in your handbag, or it's a bookmark in a book, or under the cushion, or on the worktop in the kitchen, or wherever your latest fancy takes you.'

The longer he went on, the redder her face became. 'Yes, darling,' she said, turning a page of the *Radio Times* and banging and slapping it as noisily as possible.

He glanced at her, frowned, then shook his head. He reached the sideboard and picked up the envelope. He tore it open, took out the letter and read it. His face changed. His mouth set in a grim line. 'Would you believe it? It's from the gas people. They are saying that because our boiler is over ten years old, it ought to be changed because if anything went wrong with it they may not be able to get the parts. Also they say that changing to a new boiler could save us up to 43 per cent off our consumption rate. Huh! What do you think to *that*?'

'Well, they might be right,' Mary said quietly.

Angel glared at her, then he screwed up the letter and threw it angrily at the hearth.

She stared at him.

'Yes and I think I saw a herd of pigs fly past the window,' he said.

Mary looked up, concerned. 'Where? What?' she said urgently.

Angel smiled down at her.

She looked up at him. With a grin, she said, 'Oh, you fool!'

It was a warm, dry, spring evening, just right for a gentle walk to shake a double helping of cottage pie and cabbage down, so Angel decided to walk the mile or so into town to Clement Attlee Square to check out the Italian double-bassist's shop. He passed a few people on the way. He arrived just as the light was failing. There was a car parked outside the Northern Bank, which was on one side of Vittorio Ramazzotti's empty shop, and a white van parked outside Gregg's newsagents, which was on the other side. Angel realized that the white van must be the one that Gregg had been complaining about. He walked round it. He peered into the cab but there was nothing to see that was out of the ordinary. The road-tax licence was in order. The tyres appeared to have adequate tread. He read off the licence plate and consigned the number to his memory. Then he went up to Vittorio Ramazzotti's shop, which had closed-down signs pasted all over the windows. The shop doorknob was smooth so he reckoned Ramazzotti used that door as his usual means of access. He stepped back and looked up at the first-floor windows and saw a light being switched on followed by the little man actually closing the curtains. Angel thought he must live there.

He looked round the square and found nothing else of interest so he turned and made for home. His mind became busy, very busy with something he had seen. If he passed any people on the way home, he didn't notice them.

It was dark when he arrived home, and Mary had already gone to bed.

He wrote the number of the white van onto the edge of the *Radio Times*, tore it off and shoved it into his pocket. He locked the door, turned off the light and went upstairs.

It was 6.30 a.m. It was pitch black. Angel's eyes clicked open. He was wide awake. He wondered what had wakened him. He listened. All he could hear was the gentle, even breathing of Mary asleep next to him.

Then his mind, in the darkness, filled with scenes of the mad Italian feverishly playing a double bass, the mysterious white van being driven away by an invisible man, and the angry newsagent Gregg jumping up and down on the pavement in front of his shop waving an *Exchange & Mart* in the air.

He peeled the duvet back gently so as not to disturb Mary, fished around on the carpet for his slippers and quietly slipped out of bed. He reached out for his dressing gown, then made his way out of the room and closed the door. He had a quick shower, a shave, then he dressed. He made himself a pot of tea and some toast which he dawdled over. He left a note under a magnet on the fridge door. It said: 'Gone to the office. Everything OK. Love you. M.'

Then he left the house and got the BMW out of the garage and drove straight to Clement Attlee Square. The sun was coming up. The town was quiet with very little traffic. He passed a big Asda van only. There were no pedestrians about. The square was deserted. The two vehicles that had been parked there earlier had gone. He stopped the BMW in the middle of the square and got out. He walked towards the place where the white van had been parked. He selected a spot in the middle of the parking space and squatted down in the road. As he looked around, he saw a pencil-thin line of soil about the length of a book, next to a metal plate about three feet by three feet set in the road which had the words 'Gas Inspection Chamber' moulded on its surface. He reached out and pressed one finger down on the soil, then drew his finger downwards making a smear mark on the ground. He rubbed his thumb against his finger to try to clean off the earth.

His eyebrows lowered, and his heart began to thump away. He straightened up from the crouching position and returned to the BMW. He sat in the car rubbing his chin. After a few minutes, he dived into his pocket for his mobile and tapped in a number. It was to the Firearms Special Unit in Wakefield. He wanted to speak to Detective Inspector Waldo White. They were old friends.

'Sorry to ring so early, Waldo,' Angel said into the phone.

'It's not early for us, Michael,' he replied. 'We are on duty 24/7. What's up?'

'I have a situation developing here, Waldo, and later today, I may need some of your specialist brand of muscle.'

'I can be there in about twenty-five minutes.'

'Great stuff,' Angel said and he ended the call, closed the phone and put it in his pocket. Then he started the engine and drove the BMW to the police station.

As he parked the car in his usual marked-out parking spot, near the rear entrance, he looked at his watch. It was 8.27 a.m.

As he came down the corridor, he looked into the CID room and found Ahmed taking off his coat.

'Ahmed,' he said.

He turned round. 'Good morning, sir. Did you want something?'

'Yes, lad. I want you to find Sergeants Carter, Crisp, and Taylor, and DC Scrivens and tell them I want to see them in the briefing room ASAP on a matter of extreme urgency. All right?'

'Oh yes, sir,' Ahmed said and he reached out for the phone with a free hand.

'Keep on it, lad, until all four have been contacted, and I want you to come in as well. Oh yes,' he added as he reached into his pocket and pulled out the piece of paper on which he had scrawled the white van's number. 'Will you find out who owns this vehicle? It's a large white Ford van.'

'Right, sir.'

Angel then turned away and made for his office.

About twenty minutes later, assembled in the briefing room at Bromersley station, were Angel, Flora Carter, Crisp, Taylor, Scrivens, Ahmed Ahaz and DI Waldo White. Ahmed was last in. He looked round to see that everybody was present, then he closed the door.

'Everybody's here, sir.' Ahmed said.

'Right, lad,' Angel said. Then he looked around at the expectant faces. 'Sit down, everybody, please. Anywhere. Quick as you can.'

The seven were seated in an informal semi-circle so that everybody could see everybody else.

Angel began.

'Thank you all for responding so promptly. I give special thanks and a warm welcome to DI White of the FSU for coming over from Wakefield.

'Today Lord Tulliver will be opening the International Jewellery Fair in Leeds at ten o'clock. Accompanying him will be Lady Tulliver wearing the Mermaid Diamond. I don't need to spend any time talking about its worth, the papers have been full of it, nor to suggest what an attraction it will be to every thief in the world. I understand that there will be a highly respected firm looking after the general security of the fair and that there will be a number of West Yorkshire plain-clothes police there. Some insurance companies will, no doubt, also have their men watching over their more significant clients. I also understand that the hall, the public rooms and corridors will be monitored by CCTV. So I wouldn't expect a large-scale robbery to be attempted in the building.

'However, the most valuable single jewel on view today, the Mermaid Diamond, is kept in the Northern Bank in Clement Attlee Square here in Bromersley when it is not being worn, and because of several apparently separate incidents over the past two weeks or so, I believe that tonight an attempt will be made on the vault of the Northern Bank. For the last three weeks or more I believe that a gang has been burrowing alongside a pipeline which they have cleverly entered through a gas inspection chamber cover in a parking area of Clement Attlee Square. They have then tunnelled under a shop, which was a music shop, to the building next door, which is the bank, and that they now have an explosive device set close to the wall of the vault ready to detonate to allow them to make a quick entry and exit. I believe that when the Tullivers have returned the diamond later today and the bank is closed for business, the gang will strike. After 8 p.m. tonight is the most likely time, because they would then have the benefit of darkness in which to make their escape.

'It will have been an expensive robbery for the gang to mount, so I expect they will be armed. That is why I have asked our friends, the FSU, to assist us in this operation.

'The plan that DI White and I have devised is this. Firstly, the gang may well be attempting to monitor the collecting of the diamond for Lady Tulliver this morning. They will want to clock who actually collects it, who carries it, in which vehicle and so on. They would like to know that so that they will know who and what to look out for when it is returned to the bank's safekeeping later today. They won't want to break into the bank if the diamond is not there. And, by the way, the Mermaid Diamond will have to be collected very shortly because her ladyship has to arrive in Leeds wearing it and looking fabulous by around 9.45 or so to be on time at the opening, advertised to be at ten o'clock.

'So we need to set up an "obbo" quickly from where we can keep an eye on the square and align two video cameras to film the activity around the front entrance of the bank and the gas inspection chamber on the road in front of Gregg's shop. A ground or first-floor room in a house opposite the square on Bradford Road would be ideal. And that needs organizing right now.'

He looked down the line at DS Crisp. 'Will you see to that, Trevor?'

'Right, sir,' Crisp said.

Angel said, 'There must be somebody on that stretch of road who will cooperate. You have no time to waste. Off you go. Take Ted Scrivens with you. And when you are all set up give me a ring.'

'Right, sir,' Crisp said, and he and Scrivens hurried out of the room.

'Obviously, we want to arrest *all* the gang, if possible,' Angel said, 'and as we have the element of surprise, don't let's lose it. Does anybody here have an account at the Royal Westminster branch in Clement Attlee Square?'

DS Carter said, 'I do, sir. Just an ordinary cheque account.'

Angel smiled. 'Great stuff. Can you go there and see what you can see inside the building, particularly when Lord Tulliver – or whoever it might be – arrives to collect the diamond? Also to see if there is any sign of criminal activity inside the bank that might be useful for us to know about ... familiar faces, for instance.'

'Yes, sir,' Flora Carter said. 'But it's a bit difficult hanging around without being conspicuous.'

'You *mustn't* be conspicuous, lass. I'll tell you what, tell them you want to buy a house and see if you can get them to grant you a loan. If and when they make you a proposal, ask a lot of questions. That should keep you in there for an hour at least, but don't stay any longer than that. Keep your eyes peeled and let me know if you see anything helpful.'

'I will, sir,' she said, then she hurried out.

'Right,' Angel said, 'now the rest of us will assemble from 20.00 hours in unmarked cars in strategic positions out of sight of the bank, but all within a few seconds' drive of Clement Attlee Square. Our cue will come some little time after the bank alarm bells ring, when the gang will have broken through the vault wall, found the diamond and filled their pockets with as much other loot as they can carry, made their way back along the tunnel to the gas inspection chamber, climbed up into the van through a specially made access hole cut through the bottom of their van, replaced the grate over the gas inspection chamber and the van begins to move away. Trevor Crisp will – hopefully – be observing the van from the "obbo" and will alert us. Then we move in. We should allow them to pull away from their parking place so that we have the best chance of catching them *all*.'

'After the gang's broken into the vault, the alarm will be ringing like fury, so they won't hang about. We don't know what time today they will enter the tunnel. They will need to be parked over the gas inspection chamber in good time so that they don't lose their specific loading and unloading position. I was thinking that it might be possible to put a transmitting marker on the van so that if anything goes wrong we would always be able to find it.'

'It would be a risky business, Michael,' DI White said. 'If we were seen ...'

Angel looked pensive. 'Yes,' he said with a nod. 'All right. There should be enough of us not to allow it to get away. Right. Are there any questions?'

'Yes, sir,' Taylor said. 'Shouldn't we tell the Tullivers that we believe that the bank is going to be robbed tonight and that—'

'No,' Angel said. 'If we did that, all their protective security measures would come into play. They would be doubling their security guard, their insurance company would be jumping up and down, Lady Tulliver would have a touch of the vapours and the robbers might suspect a trap. We want everything to seem normal.'

'I agree,' DI White said. 'If the gang has the slightest suspicion that anything is amiss, they might delay the project or abandon it altogether, and the opportunity to catch them might be gone for a long time.'

'This project is top secret,' Angel said. 'We tell nobody about it until it is over. Is that understood?'

'Yes, sir,' Taylor and Ahmed said.

'Anything else?'

'Yes, sir,' Taylor said. 'Does this mean that we'll be working tonight?'

'Yes, lad. Does that interfere with your plans?'

'Oh no, sir,' he said with a cheeky grin. 'Glad to get some overtime in, with summer holidays coming up.'

'If there's nothing else, Don, don't wander far today. Don't leave the station.'

'Right, sir,' he said and he went out.

Angel turned to Ahmed. 'What about that van, lad? Did you find out who owns it?'

'Yes, sir. The owners are J. P. Sorenson Limited. It's a commercial van hire company, sir, Bayswater Road, London. I've spoken to Mr Sorenson and he says that it's on hire to a Mr Edward Oliver for three months.'

Angel's heart missed a beat. His pulse began to race. That name kept cropping up in all bad, very bad places. His lips tightened back against his teeth. He ran his hand smoothly over his hair. 'Are you sure he said "Edward Oliver", Ahmed?'

'Oh yes, sir.'

'Have you a phone number for the firm?'

'I'll soon get it, sir,' Ahmed said and rushed off.

DI Waldo White saw Angel change colour and he came over. 'What's the matter, Michael? Anything I can do to help?'

'No. I don't think so. I'm investigating a murder case and the name, which is an alias, is the name of the murderer. Ahmed has just told me that, according to the owner of the white van, it was hired by a man called Edward Oliver. That damned name keeps on coming up … everywhere I turn.'

'Oh, I see. No. Sorry I can't help.'

'And the annoying thing is that I believe that I *must* know him. But I can't for the life of me place him.'

'Don't let it get to you, Michael. I know you. You'll unravel the whole thing. You always do.'

Angel sighed, then he said, 'Thanks for that vote of confidence.' Then he smiled and said, 'I'm forgetting my manners. You'll be ready for coffee, aren't you?'

'Normally, Michael, I'd snap your hand off at this time in the morning, but I'd better get back. Lots to do. See you at around 7.30 with my squad.'

'Look forward to it, Waldo,' Angel said with a wave of the hand. White had gone.

Angel followed him out of the briefing room, but went down the corridor to his own office.

Ahmed followed him in, waving what looked like a page torn out of his notebook. He pushed the slip of paper under Angel's nose and said, 'That phone number, sir.'

'Ah. Right, lad. Thank you.'

Ahmed went out.

Angel tapped the London exchange number into his phone. He was soon speaking to Mr John Percy Sorenson, head of J. P. Sorenson Limited. Angel gave him the number of the white van in question and said that he understood that it had been hired to an Edward Oliver for three months.

'Yes, that's right, Inspector,' Sorensen said. 'As I remember he was a very charming man.'

Angel pursed his lips. 'You wouldn't let a stranger hire one of your vans without checking that he was genuine, had a permanent address and that he was a responsible driver, would you?'

'Certainly not, but we can't check everything, Inspector. We check as much as we can, of course. I am looking at his application form now. Mmm. It seems to read all right.'

'Could you email a copy of it to me, Mr Sorensen?'

'Of course. I will have that done straightaway.'

'Thank you very much. Now, can you describe him?'

'Well, he was … I tell you, the girls in the office almost swooned when he came in. He was tall, slim, dark hair and a bit … erm, puckish, you know, I suppose …'

Angel thought he knew exactly what Sorensen intended to say. 'Do you mean he had a cherubic face?'

'Yes. That's it, precisely,' Sorensen said.

Angel's heart began to pound like a mechanical sledgehammer. The man's description confirmed that it was the same creature who'd murdered Nancy Quinn and Ernest Piddington. It now seemed he was also involved in the plan to steal the Mermaid Diamond. Angel wrinkled his nose. It seemed that wherever there was dishonesty, Edward Oliver was at the forefront. Was there no end to this man's wickedness?

'How was he dressed?' Angel said.

'Very smartly. Well-cut dark suit, collar and tie, as I remember.'

'Thank you very much, Mr Sorensen. One last question ... Do you remember anything particularly striking about him?'

There was a short pause. 'No,' Sorensen said. 'He was the personification of a successful, straightforward businessman, Inspector. But why all these questions? Is he wanted for something? I hope my rental will be all right.'

'We just need to speak to him about something, that's all,' Angel said evenly. He didn't want Sorenson making waves until all the thieves had been caught. 'I look forward to receiving a copy of that application form,' he added.

Angel ended the call and put the phone into its holster. He bit his lip as he considered again the possibility – nay, the certainty almost – that the person behind the name 'Edward Oliver' was also involved in the planned robbery of the Northern Bank. He shouldn't have been surprised: Edward Oliver was a highly skilled academic with a sick and convoluted mind. He must have been to be able to devise a complex scheme to persuade a man to leave his home by selling him a tomfool fairy story about double-bass music parts needing to be rewritten, the ruse being conceived solely to allow the crooks to tunnel under the man's house without having to consider the noise they might make. They had probably used powered hand tools for the heavy work. They would be noisy and may have created vibrations.

The phone rang. He picked it up. 'Angel.'

'It's Flora, sir,' she said in a whisper. 'I'm sitting in the open office part of the bank, being attended to by a young woman. She's just gone off to check on my record. I can see pretty well everybody who comes in and goes out. Two men in Astra Security uniforms, carrying their helmets, have just come in. They went up to the counter and rang the bell. A young girl came and they passed her an envelope. The clerk has taken it. Hold on, sir.'

'Right. While I'm holding on, did you happen to see whether the white van was parked up outside Gregg's?'

'Yes, sir, it was.'

'When you leave the bank be aware that there will almost certainly be eyes in the van watching everything that is happening.'

'Don't worry, sir, I'll be careful. Oh, the clerk has just come back. She's got an older man with her. He's said something to them. Both security men are looking surprised. They are searching their pockets. Oh, I see. Looks like the bank official wanted more ID from them. He's checking it.... Hold on, sir.... It seems he's satisfied. He's produced a book.... Oh I see. He wants their signatures. He's handed them a small black tin box. Looks as if it could contain the Mermaid Diamond. What do you want me to do now?'

'Wait until they leave. Unobtrusively follow them outside, clock the scene, then come back here.'

He ended the call, but it rang again. It was Crisp.

'We've set up our obbo in a first-floor bedroom of number 16, Bradford Road, sir, so we've got great views of the front entrance of the Northern Bank and the white Ford van in front of Gregg's. And both cameras are running as we speak. As a matter of fact, I've just seen an Astra Security van arrive with four men inside and … no, the two men who got out are returning now and getting back into the van.'

'Are they carrying anything?'

'Can't see too well, sir. Just let me get my binoculars on them. Mmmm. Yes. Looks like one of them is carrying a small black book or parcel.'

'Could it be a black tin deed box?'

Crisp suddenly sounded animated. 'Yes. A deed box,' he said. '*That* could be the diamond, sir ... and there's Flora Carter just coming out of the bank. She's walking between Gregg's and the white van as if she was on a holiday stroll on Blackpool promenade.'

Angel smiled. 'Right, lad,' he said.

Then he ended the call, closed the phone, sighed and leaned back in his chair.

SEVENTEEN

It was about an hour later the same morning, that Angel remembered that he had not heard lately from his old friend Dr Mac, who might have some vital information, so he picked up the phone and tapped in the Bromersley General Hospital number and was eventually put through to the mortuary.

The doctor's familiar Glaswegian voice came on the line. 'Good morning, Michael. Long time since I heard from you. Must be a whole week. I was beginning to think you'd come into money and retired to live in the Maldives.'

'I won't be able to do that – even if I wanted to – unless I could earn what a nerdy pathologist I know, who lives, breathes and dreams dead bodies, earns, and only considers humans in terms of what they might look like opened up on a slab.'

'*My*, we are in a mood this morning, laddie. Let me see if I can cheer you up.'

'You won't cheer me up if you haven't got answers, Mac,' Angel said.

'Well, what is it you want to know?'

'The last I heard was that you thought that whoever murdered Nancy Quinn did it with a short-bladed knife, probably a common-or-garden steak knife.'

'That's right, Michael. There were twenty-eight separate stabbing wounds in her thorax, abdomen, pelvis and chest.'

'And that it was probably committed during intercourse.'

'That's right.'

'So were you able to locate any semen for DNA purposes?'

'No. Not in this case. I suspect the man was barren. That often goes along with being a psychotic patient. He needs finding and locking up, Michael, and quickly.'

Angel blew out a length of air. 'Couldn't agree with you more, but I need evidence, Mac. And you're not helping.'

'Sorry, Michael. That's the best I can do.'

Angel thanked the pathologist, ended the call and then tapped in another number. There was a knock on the door.

He called out, 'Come in.'

It was Don Taylor with a large brown registered envelope.

Angel saw the envelope and his face brightened. He cancelled the call and dropped the phone into its holster.

'You've got some results, Don?'

'From Wetherby lab, sir. The DNA results of ten different hair samples. Eight were from different pieces of clothing in Nancy Quinn's wardrobe, one was from her stomach and the other from her thigh. The DNA of one of the eight hairs from her clothes matches both hairs taken from her body. The rest are all different. However, I have checked all the DNA on the PNC, and it is all negative.'

His face dropped. 'That's not much use, then. Of course, not every villain's DNA is on the PNC. The only thing it tells us is that her murderer was all over her. But we knew that. We need the DNA of Edward Oliver – or whatever his name is – to *prove* it was him.'

Taylor went out and Angel picked up the phone.

There was a knock on the door. Angel glared at it. 'Come in,' he called.

It was Ahmed. He was holding two sheets of A4.

Angel frowned, looked at what he had in his hand and said, 'Is that from Sorensen's?'

'Just come through by email, sir.'

Angel slammed the phone down into its holster. 'I have been trying to ring you about that,' he said taking the two sheets of paper from him.

Angel read each entry of the application form to hire a vehicle which, of course, was in the name of Edward Oliver and entirely fictitious. The crook would have had to answer each question exactly so as to match the entries in a driving licence he must have shown to Mr Sorensen which itself must have been a forgery. Angel noticed the date of birth, 14 March 1971, and wondered whether in a thoughtless moment it was possible the crook might have entered his own actual date of birth or had he just pulled a date entirely out of thin air?

He conveyed this thought to Ahmed.

'I'll go back to the PNC site, sir and tap that date in and see if it throws any names up.'

'Great stuff,' Angel said. 'We are due a bit of luck, Ahmed. Off you go, then.'

As Ahmed closed the door, Angel picked up the phone and entered in a number. It was his own home number. He wanted to speak to Mary. He wanted to tell her about tonight. She wouldn't be pleased.

'Hello,' she said in a voice that sounded interested and welcoming, whoever it was.

Angel adopted a cheerful attitude. 'Hello, sweetheart,' he said, 'just rung to say – in plenty of time, you may note – that I won't be home till late tonight. There's an exercise I have to attend.'

Mary wasn't pleased. 'What sort of exercise?'

'A field exercise for the young PCs, nothing to worry about. I might not get home until midnight.'

'Midnight? Oh. And what about your tea?'

'Erm. I'll have it tomorrow.'

'And what about tomorrow's tea?

Angel was losing his patience. 'I'll have that the day after. What is all this? Puzzle corner? I'm giving you loads of notice because we have this exercise thrust upon us. I can't help it. But it's nothing to worry about.'

'I hope this is not going to become a regular thing.'

'Of course it isn't. If there's anything good on the telly, you can record it for me. I think there's a new episode of *Downton Abbey* on ITV.'

'What? No, there isn't. And anyway, would you expect me to watch it twice? And what are you going to do about your tea?'

'I'll be all right. I'll get something from the pub.'

'Huh, the pub. You don't want to be hanging around there for long.'

'If I'm not home by eleven or so, lock up and go to bed.'

'You'd better be in by midnight.'

He knocked imperatively on the desk. 'Got to go, love. Somebody at the door. If I can, love, I will. If I can't, I won't. And anyway, I'll see you in the morning.' Then he added tenderly, 'Goodbye and take care.'

There was the slightest pause, then Mary gently said, 'Goodbye and you take care.'

He smiled, cancelled the call, shook his head and dropped the phone in the holster.

Angel was busy at his desk and was disturbed by a knock on the door.

'Come in,' he called.

'It's 7.25, sir,' Ahmed said, 'and DI White's here.'

'Right, lad,' Angel said, throwing down his pen. 'Get Sergeants

Carter and Taylor. We want to be ready in five minutes. Have you told your mother you are working late?'

Ahmed grinned. 'Oh, yes, sir.'

Angel nodded and then jerked his head towards the door, indicating that he should leave.

Ahmed went out and held the door open for DI White.

'Come in, Waldo,' Angel said. 'Right on time.'

White grinned. 'Good evening, Michael. So the diamond has been duly returned to the bank and there has been no visible movement of the robbers.'

Angel nodded. 'It should be a straightforward procedure, Waldo.'

It was two o'clock on the morning of Wednesday, 15 May. The south Yorkshire town of Bromersley was quiet, still and as black as fingerprint ink. There were five unmarked police cars parked among other cars, each on a different backstreet, and each one no further than seconds away from the Northern Bank in Clement Attlee Square.

Angel was in his own car with Flora Carter and two other armed officers. He was on an open RT line to Crisp at the observation post on Bradford Road and the four cars. All points were keeping silence.

Suddenly, the quiet and peace of the night was disturbed by the shrill scream of alarm bells from the bank.

'There she goes,' Angel said into the phone. 'Can you hear that, Trevor?'

'Yes, sir,' Crisp said.

'And have you still got clear vision of the white van?'

'Yes, sir. And I'll keep my night vision binoculars on it until it moves.'

Angel said, 'All cars, I expect it will be a few minutes before the thieves can make their escape. Take your cue from DS Crisp. Over to you, Trevor.'

'Thank you, sir,' Crisp said. 'Two men have arrived. They're looking up at the bell on the front of the bank. They've turned away and are walking quickly up Bradford Road.... A few bedroom lights have gone on ... a car has arrived and has parked outside the front of the bank.... '

Crisp maintained the commentary for ten minutes or so, then suddenly he stopped, drew in air loudly enough to be heard through the RT in all five cars, his voice went up an octave and he said, 'It's moving. The white van is moving. All cars, go, go, go!'

From five different directions, the five unmarked police cars raced to Clement Attlee Square and quickly surrounded the white van as it pulled out into Bradford Road. The van driver tried to squeeze the van between two of the cars, but crashed dramatically into the side of one of them, damaging the bodywork extensively and stalling the van engine, which he feverishly tried to restart but failed.

The FSU police got out of their cars first and repeatedly yelled, 'Police. Put your hands where we can see them. You are surrounded.'

Then they pulled their Heckler and Koch G36 rifles into position and formed a ring round the van. Plain-clothes men mounted powerful lights on top of their cars and directed their beams onto the van.

Flora Carter was on her mobile to the station. 'Ahmed, send the Black Maria, a low loader and a tow truck to Bradford Road, opposite Clement Attlee Square, as soon as you can.'

DI White pointed his Glock G17 pistol and a powerful hand torch at the front off-side door of the van as Angel slid it open. It revealed a huge man in overalls with his hands up, blinking in the powerful lights. Behind him were five other faces of men who knew their bid for quick, easy money was now lost.

White looked at the man in the driving seat. 'Get out,' he said. 'Put your hands on top of the van.'

Angel patted him down. He felt something hard in a pocket. He took it out. It was a small matte-blue handgun. A Beretta. He looked at it closely. It was a 3032 Tomcat. Deadly at close range. Angel handed it to Flora Carter, who put it in an EVIDENCE bag and recorded it on a clipboard. PC Weightman handcuffed the prisoner and held him by the cuffs, awaiting the arrival of the Black Maria.

White instructed another of the gang to get out of the van to be searched.

At the same time, from the direction of Clement Attlee Square, Angel heard a powerful car engine suddenly roar into life. He looked round, concerned that one of the gang might have escaped. He could see nothing as the sound slowly faded into the night.

Minutes later the Black Maria arrived in Clement Attlee Square and the six men in handcuffs were taken across the road and loaded into it. One of DI White's vehicles and six of the team of twelve escorted the vehicle back to Bromersley Police Station.

The other six FSU men went with Angel and White to the gas inspection chamber and opened the lid. Two men suitably clad in denims and armed with Glock handguns and torches came forward. Angel shone his torch into the gaping mouth of the tunnel. Something small reflected back at him. It was a bright yellow colour.

He turned to White and said, 'What's that?'

'Don't know,' White said.

One of the men saw it, and reaching down, pulled it out of the damp earth and handed it up to him.

'Thank you, lad,' Angel said.

It was a gold chain with a star-shaped pendant with a circle in the middle. The diamond was missing.

Angel's eyes shone. He turned to White and said, 'It's the setting of the Mermaid Diamond!'

White realized the significance of the find.

'You two chaps,' he said, 'Keep a lookout for a big diamond on your journey, will you?'

'Yes, of course, sir.'

The two men began their journey. Initially, the tunnel was a gradual descent at around sixty degrees. After about twelve feet the tunnel levelled out and there was room to turn and crawl on hands and knees for twenty yards or so, then a gradual ascent of about six feet. The men could hear the burglar alarm that was still ringing as they approached the hole in the three-foot-thick wall of the bank's vault. The leader shone his torch inside the vault. All he could see were metal cupboards, one with its door open, and stashed with currency wrapped in cellophane packets. And there were piles of deed boxes of various shapes and sizes, maybe a hundred in all. There was no sign of anybody in there, or in the tunnel, so the men turned round and returned to the surface. The journey there and back took only a matter of five or six minutes.

Angel and White were waiting to greet them.

'Nobody down there, sir, and no sign of the diamond,' the leader said.

A disappointed Angel thanked them.

They put the cover back over the gas inspection chamber, and Angel left two PCs to guard it.

Everybody except the two PCs then returned to Bromersley nick.

The prisoners were now safely in cells and Crisp and Flora were preparing to take their fingerprints.

Angel turned to White and said, 'Well, thank you very much,

Waldo. Three more guns off the streets. And two deadly-looking knives. That was a neat job, well done, don't you think?'

White smiled. 'Glad to be of service, Michael.' He turned to go, but he came back. 'Sorry you didn't find that ... diamond?'

'The Mermaid Diamond?' The corners of Angel's mouth turned downwards. 'We haven't properly searched the prisoners.' Then he added sternly, 'I will have them X-rayed if necessary.'

White smiled. 'Good luck with that, Michael.'

'Thanks again, Waldo. I'm glad that nobody was hurt in this exercise.'

'So am I. Goodnight, Michael.'

White bustled down the corridor to round up his men in the police car park to mount their two trucks and head back to Wakefield.

Meanwhile Angel's team strip-searched the prisoners and found that they had many thousands of pounds' worth of notes stuffed in their pockets and tucked under their clothing, but the diamond was not found. They were fingerprinted and asked their names, addresses and for an explanation for their presence in a van at that time of night and other preliminary questions, but each one simply said, 'No comment' to each question.

A low loader returned to the station having picked up the Ford van wrapped in plastic sheets and tied with rope for forensic examination later that morning; also a tow truck that had been sent to collect the damaged police car was delivered to the garage.

It was 4 a.m. before the prisoners had been examined by the police doctor, interviewed, satisfactorily fed, watered, safely housed for the night and could be left in charge of the duty sergeant.

Angel checked with each of his team members and thanked them for their work and they left for their homes. He called in on the night-duty desk sergeant.

'Are you off, sir?' Clifton said.

'Yes, Bernie. They should be all right until morning.'

Clifton smiled. 'It's been a great coup for you, sir. Six villains at a stroke.'

Angel smiled weakly. 'I suppose so.'

'I bet you'll sleep like a top tonight, sir, what's left of it.'

'Aye,' he said as he put on his coat.

'You get off, sir. If anything comes up, I'll push it onto Inspector Asquith.'

'Thanks, Bernie. Goodnight.'

'Goodnight, sir.'

Buoyed up by the arrest of the six robbers and the desk sergeant's positive comments, Angel went out of the station front door and skipped down the steps to the pavement. But the cool morning air made him suddenly feel tired, and as he reached the BMW, he was thinking that the night had not really been entirely a success. He hadn't found the Mermaid Diamond.

EIGHTEEN

It was 8.28 a.m. on Wednesday morning. Angel walked down the corridor as usual. He went into his office and began taking off his coat. The alarm had woken him at 7.30 as always and he had to force himself but here he was. He had had three hours' sleep. He should have had longer, but there was too much on his mind. He had to find that diamond.

There was a knock on the door.

'Come in,' he called. The door opened and it was Ahmed.

Angel's eyebrows shot up. 'I told you there was no need to come in until ten o'clock or so …'

'I know, sir,' Ahmed said, 'but my mother asked me if *you* would be in as usual. Of course, I had to say yes, so she said, well then, I should be there at the same time too. Then she said, you can go to bed straight from work today and sleep around the clock all night tonight to catch up if you need to. So, well sir, here I am.'

Angel smiled. Then shook his head.

Ahmed said, 'And I have to report that nobody registered on the PNC was born on 14 March 1971.'

Angel frowned.

Ahmed said, 'Yesterday morning, sir, you asked me to check on the PNC to see if anybody there was born on that day. This was the entry on Edward Oliver's application to hire a van, don't you remember? It was a long shot, but …'

'I do now, lad,' he said, with his nose pushed up and his lips with it. 'Another dead end. This case has nothing but dead ends.'

The phone rang. Angel looked at it, then turned back to Ahmed and said, 'Get Don Taylor to look at that white van that was brought in last night ASAP, will you?'

'Right, sir,' Ahmed said and he went out.

He picked up the phone. 'Angel,' he said.

Angel heard a loud and long noise that he recognized and detected was Superintendent Harker clearing his throat. Then he heard Harker say, 'Ah yes, Angel, I want you up here ASAP.' It was followed by a loud click as Harker slammed down his phone.

Angel sighed. He had no idea what he wanted, but he didn't expect to be congratulated on last night's arrests. Trips to his office were very rarely pleasant. He made his way up the corridor to the last door on the end. He knocked on the door, pushed it open and entered.

It was like a sauna inside. But instead of the smell of aloe vera or lavender, it was menthol.

Harker, partly hidden by piles of ledgers, papers and files on his desk, stuck his head forward and said, 'Ah, *there* you are, lad. What on earth have you done? I've just had the manager of the Northern Bank on the phone, reporting a burglary. Now, the Northern Bank is my bank. I've been banking there for nearly thirty-six years. I don't want you upsetting him. He says that a constable attending said that DI Angel was already on the case. He said that you had been on the case even before the alarm went off at 02.02 this morning. He's upset because he wasn't informed and he wasn't called out.'

Angel had expected trouble. That's all visits to this office were. He didn't reply. He waited for the question to be put into context.

Harker continued: 'And this station has more guests to feed than the Feathers. *Six* of them. What's going on?'

'These men have been charged with stealing the Mermaid Diamond, sir.'

Harker blinked, then frowned. 'Oh. My goodness. Do you mean the big one, the colossal one? The one that Lady Tulliver wears? I didn't realize it had been stolen.'

'Yes, sir. And my team have arrested a gang. You wanted a gang, sir, or that's what I thought you had said.'

'Oh, dear me. Well, you'd better put it somewhere very safe. It would be better to deposit it in a bank and get a receipt for it. The insurance we have here wouldn't cover it. Oh, my goodness me. No.'

Angel shuffled in the chair and the corners of his mouth were turned down. 'I haven't actually *found* the diamond, sir,' he said.

'What did you say, lad?'

'I said that I haven't yet located the diamond, sir,' he said.

'Well, what are we boarding six men for? Have you a case against them or not?'

'Yes, sir. The case against them is that they *conspired* to *steal* the diamond.'

'And you can prove it?'

Angel had to think quickly. He wasn't sure that he could prove it. He swiftly changed tack. 'They are also charged with breaking into a bank and stealing – between them – £720,000,' he said.

'You have recovered that money, I hope?'

'Yes, sir,' Angel said. 'It's in the station safe.'

'Hmm. I see that we have an unmarked patrol car out of service. I saw it as I came in this morning. How we are to manage without it, I really don't know.'

'It was unavoidable, sir. The robbers' van was surrounded by our vehicles and the driver rammed his van into our car in a bid to escape. In no way was our driver to blame.'

'It still means we will be one car short for goodness knows how long. And we shall have a heavy bill for the repairs. And your team will be putting overtime chits in, I expect? *There's* another expense.'

'They all did a very good job, sir. I also had to call in the FSU, sir.'

'The FSU?' he said, raising his bushy ginger eyebrows. 'Dearie me, Angel. It gets worse. This operation is turning into a very expensive night out. How I keep this station within its budget, I don't know. And it looks as if you didn't catch the top man in this gang. I expect he escaped with the stone and we'll never see it or him ever again.'

Angel's fists clenched. He knew this was a serious possibility.

Harker said, 'If ever you have to mount an expensive operation like this again, I need to know *before* you commit the force to such needless extravagance.'

Angel shook his head. He didn't think it was by any means an expensive operation. 'There was no needless extravagance here, sir. We needed the FSU. The robbers were dangerously armed. We took three guns off them and two knives so we certainly needed armed support.'

'But you failed to recover the diamond. The whole object of the exercise!'

Angel didn't have a satisfactory answer to the superintendent on that point so he said nothing.

Harker saw that he was not answering. 'The trouble with you, Angel, is that your head is too big. You think that because you've had your name in the paper a few times and had articles written about you that that makes you a genius, and God's gift to the police force. Well, let me acquaint you with the real situation: you are not. You bumble your way from one investigation to another, eventually falling over a solution. And hey presto! Like a conjuror pulling a rabbit out of a hat, you appear to have solved the crime.

Now, I know you've always solved the cases you've been given in the past, but your good luck has to come to an end. And this case looks like being the one to do it. Now buzz off and find that diamond, if you can, without incurring this station in any more wasteful and unnecessary expense.'

Angel came out of Harker's office fuming. He stormed back down to his office, and met DS Carter at the door.

'What do you want, lass? And what are you doing here anyway? I told everybody on last night's op there was no need to come in until ten o'clock.'

She shrugged. 'Do you want me to go home?' she said with a grin.

'No. Not now you're here. Come in. I must just make this call to Don Taylor.'

They went into his office. He reached out for the phone and tapped in a single digit.

'Don, have you started on that white van yet?'

'We are just unwrapping it now, sir.'

'It is possible that one of the thieves hid the diamond pendant somewhere in the bodywork or under the upholstery. The same is possible in the Black Maria. Will you give both vehicles a very, very close search and let me know instantly if you find anything?'

'Right, sir.'

He closed the phone, replaced it and turned to Carter. 'Now, Flora, what did you want?'

Before she could reply, the phone rang. He reached out for it. 'Angel.'

A rich, but menacing voice of an educated man who thought he was a superior being said, 'I left a message for you.'

It was the voice of the person Angel knew as Edward Oliver.

Angel's blood ran cold. His pulse began to race. He held his breath. But he had the presence of mind to press the record button on the telephone.

The voice continued: 'The message said, "Inspector A – don't get in my way." It was left in red. Have you forgotten it already?'

Flora knew that something was wrong. They exchanged glances. Angel snatched up his pen and scribbled on the paper nearest to him, 'Trace this call.' Then he turned it towards her, she read it, nodded and rushed out of the office.

'Are you there?' the voice said. 'I see that I have your attention.'

His voice was like icicles Angel had seen hanging from the roof outside latrines at Strangeways.

'I am here all right, Mr Oliver. Who are you and what do you want?'

'You defied me, Angel,' the voice continued, 'yes, you defied me. Not only did you stop me from getting the money Piddington had stolen from the bank, but you also tried to stop me getting the Mermaid Diamond. Nobody pulls two strokes across me and gets off scot-free. Oh no. Now, Angel, I have a young woman here, a very beautiful young woman, who wants to speak to you. I don't know if I should let her. Hold on, I'll see if she wants to be nice to me. If she does, I'll let her speak to you.'

Angel's heart was beating so strongly, he thought it might break out through his shirt. He couldn't imagine who he could mean.

'Who is it, you bastard?' Angel said. 'Who is it?'

He didn't have to wait long to find out.

'Michael. Oh Michael, darling,' she said.

It was Mary. His beloved wife.

'This man is wearing a black hood,' she said.

Every muscle in Angel's body tightened. The monster had Mary in his clutches.

'I am here, Mary,' he said. 'Where are you?'

'I have no idea who he is. I beg of you, do as he says. He says he'll kill me if you tell anyone there, but you're to look at the CD in the computer at home.'

'Mary,' Angel began. But the phone call had abruptly ended.

Inside, his chest was burning like a furnace. It felt as if it would burst. He had never known that he loved Mary so much. He dropped the phone and ran out to his car.

Flora saw him fly past her on the corridor. She saw his face and knew something was very wrong. She went into his office, saw the phone thrown down on the desk. She picked it up and put it to her ear. There was nothing. Then she remembered that he had pressed the record button. She pressed the green playback button and listened to the conversation he had had with the man only three minutes ago. She was shocked when she heard the playback. She couldn't decide what to do. She knew she couldn't do nothing. She decided to race after him and offer to help despite the threat. She put the phone back in its holster and rushed out to the car park. She knew his first stop would be his home to play the CD.

Angel drove the BMW like a madman. He saw only what was directly ahead in his path. He arrived at home in record time. He dashed into the unlocked house and went straight into the sitting room where the computer was set up on a bureau in an alcove at the side of the fireplace. He switched it on and impatiently waited for it to go through its processes. In the computer tower was a drawer for CDs. He pressed the button and the drawer came out with a disc on it. He glanced at the disc. It had a blank label unfamiliar to him. That must be the one.

He was about to play it when he heard a noise in the hallway. He gasped. Every nerve in his body tightened.

It was Flora Carter.

'Oh, it's you,' he said.

'I followed you.'

He shook his head and returned to the computer. He put the cursor on the start button and clicked on it.

On the screen it showed a man wearing a black hood with slot holes for eyes. He was pointing a handgun at Mary. Mary was seated with her wrists tied to the arms of a chair. Mary said, 'He wants me to say that you've to look in slot 212 in the bird's waterproof.'

Then the computer screen went black.

'Look in slot 212 in the bird's waterproof,' Flora said. 'It's a sort of puzzle, or conundrum ... like a crossword clue. What's it mean?'

'It *is* a crossword clue,' Angel said. His face looked grim. 'Slot 212 means a letterbox of a house or a flat. Very rare to have flats numbering up to 212. It *must* be a house number, but which street?' He ran his hand through his hair. 'There are millions of streets.'

'What's a bird's waterproof. Birds don't have waterproof coats or anything.'

'They do. Their coats. Their feathers are waterproof.'

'Oh yes ... their feathers ...'

'*The Feathers*,' he said. 'The Feathers Hotel. Slot 212. I've got it.'

He dashed out to the street to the BMW and drove off.

Flora closed down the computer, came out of the house and closed the door. She followed him to the Feathers in her own car.

Angel dashed up to the reception desk and asked if there was any mail for room 212. The clerk turned round, looked along the key slots and found one envelope. He passed it over to Angel.

Angel moved away from the desk and tore open the envelope. The single sheet of paper inside read: 'Still with us, Angel? Try this. No apples. Just water, but in a tin. RLS.'

He groaned, slumped into a seat in the reception area and stared at the paper.

Flora came in through the rotating doors, saw him and rushed over.

'There you are,' she said.

He looked up and passed her the note.

She sat down next to him and read it aloud: 'No apples. Just water, but in a tin. RLS.'

'It's a toughie,' Angel said.

'Who do you know with the initials RLS, sir?'

'I've been thinking … I can't think of anybody I've ever put away or worked with … it's a Robert, Roger, Ralph, Raymond … or to take the surname, Smith, Sunderland, Scott, Southall, Stevenson … I don't know, there must be hundreds.'

Angel rubbed his chin. 'The only name that comes to mind is Robert Louis Stevenson. But he didn't write this clue. It's not him.'

Flora closed her eyes and said, 'I can't think …'

'"No apples,"' he said, repeating the clue. 'Years ago they used to put apples in a barrel.'

'In that story …'

'*Treasure Island* by Robert Louis Stevenson.'

'That's it,' she said.

'The boy hides in an apple barrel. An apple barrel.'

'"No apples. Just water,"' she said reading the clue again.

'Does that mean a water barrel? The only water barrel I know of round here is at the vicarage.'

He dashed out of the Feathers. Flora caught up with him at the door of the BMW. 'Shall I come with you, sir?'

Abstractedly, he pointed to the nearside door of the car.

'Shall I drive?' she said.

'No.'

She got into the car.

Angel drove like a madman. Flora hung onto the seatbelt as the BMW rocked wildly from one side to the other. The car roared along Park Road, then turned right down a narrow lane and through the vicarage gates. It careered down the drive, spraying the recently laid shale like water, and stopped with a jerk at the front door. He dashed out of the car and up to the doorbell, pressed it, then without waiting for a reply, ran to the back of the house to a water barrel set up on bricks with a metal cover, designed to collect rainwater. He yanked off the cover. It was almost full. Floating on the surface of the water was a tin that had once held tobacco. He picked it out of the water, removed the lid and found inside a folded piece of paper.

Flora caught up with him. 'What's it say?'

Angel's heart sank. He had had enough of this stupid game. He wanted to get to Mary. It made him sick thinking what might be happening to her. He quickly tore open the paper. It said: 'You *are* on form, Angel. Try this – inside, but outside where it's cold, where your missives may be held in contradiction to gravity.'

He read the clue again, pulled a face like thunder, then passed the note to Flora.

'He's got me beat this time.'

'No, he hasn't, sir. You can do it.'

'It doesn't make sense. What's he mean, "Inside, but outside where it's cold"? Where is it cold?' Angel said.

'The Arctic, the Antarctic, the sea generally, cold-rooms, refrigerators …'

'It says, "Inside but outside where it's cold". Does that mean on the outside of cold-rooms and refrigerators that are *inside* a building, as opposed to the Arctic where it is cold outside?'

'I should think so, sir. Give it a try.'

'Hmmm. Well, why does it say, "outside where it's cold"?' Angel said, rubbing his chin. 'Not inside. Not inside the cold-room or the refrigerator.'

'"Where your missives may be held in contradiction to gravity,"' Flora said.

'A missive is a letter or a note or some sort of communication, isn't it? He's put the word "your", so it means my office or home or car or wherever.'

'What's "held in contradiction to gravity"?'

Angel shook his head. 'I don't even know what he means. I suppose he means something that defies gravity? But nothing defies gravity, does it?'

'Say a ball bouncing, the sponginess in the ball causes the ball to bounce up in the air. Is that defying gravity?'

'In a way it is. You could say that all aeroplanes defy gravity,' he said.

'And birds and chickens, they fly. And kangaroos, they jump.'

He wrinkled his nose. 'Not kangaroos,' he said. 'Right, Flora, what have we got now?'

'Not inside the cold-room or refrigerator, where your letters or notes are held, defying gravity, like aeroplanes, birds or chickens.'

Angel shook his head. He sighed. 'I don't know, Flora. I really don't know. While we are playing this damned silly parlour game, what's happening to Mary? That man is clearly off his head.'

'But sir, we have to solve this to get to Mary.'

He took a deep breath and said, 'Yes. All right. What have we got, then?'

Flora said, 'Not inside the cold-room or refrigerator, where your letters or notes are held, defying gravity.'

Angel suddenly said, 'I know who that Edward Oliver is. He was a freelance crossword- and puzzle-setter for newspapers and magazines. It's quite terrifying. His real name was Dennis Reville. He murdered his wife in the most cruel way … must be twelve years ago. I arrested him. He always threatened to get back at me. His brief put up a brilliant defence. He brought psychiatrists in to testify from all over the place. They said he was a psycho. The judge sent him to Wilefowle, north of the county, at Her Majesty's pleasure. Hadn't heard he'd escaped.'

'We must solve this, sir,' Flora said. 'Come on.'

'Oh yes. Outside a cold-room or refrigerator, where your letters or notes are defying gravity.'

Suddenly his eyes stopped roving around. His mouth dropped open. 'I've got it,' he said.

He ran to the driver's door of the BMW. Flora had to be quick. He pulled away before she had closed the car door.

'What does it mean, then?' she said when she had her seatbelt fastened.

'He means the next clue is under a magnet on the fridge in our kitchen!' he said as he whisked the steering wheel round to take a corner.

She nodded as her mind caught up with his explanation.

It was another scary race across Bromersley.

Eventually they arrived at his house. He dashed out of the car, leaving the door open, raced into the house to the fridge. There was a note waiting for him. He snatched it from under a magnet. It read, 'Go back two.' His eyes flashed. That must mean go back to the vicarage. He raced back to the BMW. The paper with the clue was left floating to the floor as Flora arrived in the kitchen. She saw it, picked it up, read it, then rushed out of the house.

Angel was already driving away when Flora arrived at the kerb. She stood there, mouth open, watching the BMW race down the road, and hearing the low purr of the exhaust. As he turned at the end of the street, she took out her mobile and tapped in a number.

Angel's mind was everywhere. He was frantic with worry. As the car rocked from side to side, he suddenly had a thought. He had rung the doorbell at the vicarage, and there had been no reply. Even if the vicar was out, there was his wife and his housekeeper who could have answered. He had never found the vicarage unoccupied. Even when the vicar and his wife were on holiday a covering priest from Wakefield used to stay in the house.

NINETEEN

Meanwhile inside the vicarage, Dennis Reville, the tall, dark and handsome man with the cherubic face, had been busy drilling holes in the woodwork of the sitting room and fitting up a cord threaded to the sneck on the old door then through eye-hole screws directly to the trigger of a rifle fastened to a chair and aimed directly at Mary, who was fastened to a chair by her wrists and ankles.

'You see, my dear,' Reville said to her, 'your dear husband has only to lift the sneck of the door to enter and it will tighten this cord which will pull the trigger of the rifle and you will be out of the world for good. And he will have murdered you. Isn't that a hoot?'

Mary screamed, then said, 'You'll never get away with it.'

He walked behind the chair, produced a scarf and gloves. He stuffed the gloves through her teeth.

'Oh, yes I will,' he said with a big laugh, as he tightened the scarf over her mouth and tied several knots in it. 'And your dear Michael will spend the rest of his life in torment.'

He then turned and switched on an audio tape recorder.

Angel arrived in the BMW at the vicarage, spraying the shale around the drive. He leaped out of the car and went up to the front door. He banged the Victorian knocker hard and the door opened two or three inches, as if it had not been closed properly. He pushed it open and called out, 'Anybody there? Michael Angel here! Vicar!'

A tall figure with a cherubic face peered down at him from a place in shadow beyond the curve in the stairs.

Then Angel heard a voice he knew so very well. 'Michael, help me. I'm here.' It was his beloved Mary. The voice came from the sitting room. That was the first door on the left. He entered the old house and rushed up to the door and put his hand up to the sneck to open it. Then he heard the voice again. 'Michael, help me. I'm here.' He stopped. There was something odd about the voice. It was certainly Mary, but the intonation was wrong. The call was repeated again. He realized that it was repeated every two and a half seconds. It was a recording of her voice on a loop. He looked round the door and on the floor was a sprinkling of what looked like white powder. He bent down to look at it. It was sawdust. There was something very strange. He straightened up. The recorded voice cried out again.

He continued to look at the door as the tape played Mary's voice again. Then he made a decision. He turned, went outside onto the shale and round to the sitting-room window. He peered inside and the muscles in his chest tightened as he saw Mary fastened to a chair, the rifle aimed directly at her, and the cord stretched tautly between the door and the rifle. He turned away from the window and looked around. He saw a small wooden garden seat. He dragged it towards the vicarage wall, then lifted it and threw it against the sitting-room window. There was a loud crash as the garden seat crashed into the window, causing the glass to splinter into a thousand pieces, creating a big hole in the glass. He climbed through the hole and dashed over to Mary. He firstly moved the chair holding the rifle so that she was no longer in the line of fire. He untied the scarf and she spat out the gloves.

'Oh Michael,' she said, her big eyes looking up to him. 'Are you all right?'

'I'm fine,' he said as he began to undo the rope around her wrists. 'Are *you* all right? Let's get you out of here.'

'I'm all right now, darling. But you must watch out for him. He's an evil monster.'

'I know. I know. He's as mad as a hatter. I hope he hasn't hurt you.'

'No. No,' she said.

He had finished freeing her hands and bent down to untie the rope round her ankles.

Mary suddenly saw Reville's cherubic face, looking devilish. He was now unhooded and for an instant stood just outside the window. Then he was climbing in. 'Look out, Michael. He's behind you.'

Reville leaped through the window and landed on top of the policeman, pulling him away from loosening the rope round Mary's ankles and throwing punches with clenched fists at Angel's head.

Mary looked round for something to use as a weapon against the madman, but there was nothing within her reach.

Angel managed to stand up despite the barrage of hard fists being showered on him; he was then better able to defend himself in the style of a boxer.

Reville threw a powerful left at Angel, who ducked, allowing the man to lose his balance and come towards Angel, who produced a hard left to his chin that stopped the man falling forward; Angel's punch was so powerful that Reville fell backwards to the floor. He quickly recovered and looked round for something to throw. There was a white marble bust. He grabbed it and threw it at Angel, who managed to duck and avoid it. Reville followed it through and darted towards Angel with the heavy wooden bust stand – waving it about. The stand caught the cord still draped between the door and chair. It triggered the rifle, there was a loud report and Reville collapsed to the floor. He didn't move. Angel went forward to see what had happened and discovered a bullet had entered Reville's head at his left temple. He put his hand on his neck, but could find no pulse.

'He's dead,' Angel said.

He turned away from him and returned to unfastening the rope around Mary's ankles.

There was the sound of a car door being closed. Then a face appeared at the hole in the window. It was Flora Carter. 'Is everything all right, sir?'

Angel and Mary exchanged knowing glances.

'Yes, Flora,' Angel said. 'But you'd better send for an ambulance for him.'

Dennis Reville was pronounced dead at the scene and the mortuary wagon took him away after DS Taylor and SOCO had finished their routine checks and observations.

The vicar and his wife were found gagged and bound to beds in an upstairs room. They were taken to hospital for a check-up, found to be satisfactory and safely returned home.

Flora Carter took Angel and Mary to the hospital, where several small injuries to Angel's face and head were treated and dressings applied. Apart from rope burns to her wrists, Mary was apparently unscathed. After treatment Flora took them both home.

At the front door, Angel turned to Flora and said, 'Thank you very much, lass. Now, my car is still outside the vicarage, can you pick me up in about an hour and take me to collect it?'

She smiled. 'I'll get somebody from transport to deliver it to you here ASAP, sir. How's that?'

'Even better,' he said. 'Thank you, Flora.'

He began to follow Mary into the house, then suddenly he turned back and called out, 'Oh, Flora.'

'Yes, sir?' she said, running back up the path.

Angel pursed his lips, then said, 'Reville had to have some form of transport to gad about like he's been doing. It would be useful if we can find it. He might have been using the vicar's, or he might have hired a car or stolen one. Check out the vicar's first. If it's not that, get a squad of men to look around the streets nearby. I would expect it to be in easy walking distance of the vicarage. And keep me posted.'

'Right, sir. I'll get right on it.'

He had a light lunch of soup and fruit and had a good long talk with Mary. He wanted to be sure that she was safe and sound and hadn't suffered any psychological damage at Reville's hand. Then he had a shower, changed his suit and shirt and returned to the police station.

It was 2.45 p.m. when Angel sat down at his desk. He reached out for the phone and tapped in Flora Carter's mobile number.

'Good afternoon, sir,' she said brightly. 'I hope you're feeling OK.'

'Yes, lass, thank you. Have you found that diamond?'

'No, sir, but I've quite a lot of other news.'

'I hope it's all good. Where are you?'

'I'm in the vicar's garage, sir, with Don Taylor and a couple of his officers. I'll come outside, the signal will be better.'

'Right, Flora. Fire away.'

'Well, sir, we discovered the vicar and his wife gagged and tied to their beds. They were promptly despatched to the hospital for a check-up, but I think they'll be all right. Before he went, the vicar told me that Reville knocked on the vicarage door at about nine o'clock this morning asking for help. He asked him in, then Reville drew a gun and held them at gunpoint. He demanded the keys to his garage and car, then he made them go upstairs. He fastened them to their beds with clothes line. Apparently Reville had been using the vicar's car, a small black Ford, as his own runabout this morning. The car was parked and locked in an old stable that the vicar used as a garage. It was opposite the back door of the vicarage. Don Taylor found Reville's fingerprints all over the car. The key to the garage was found in Reville's pocket together with keys for Ernest Piddington's house and Nancy Quinn's flat.'

'Good. That will help to show the free and easy way he had access to his victims.'

'I thought you'd be pleased.'

'Anything else?'

'Yes, sir. In the back of the car, under a seat, Don Taylor found a kitchen knife covered in dried blood with Reville's fingerprints on it. It was wrapped in a newspaper, which also had his prints on it.'

'Was it the *Sunday Telegraph*?'

'Yes, sir. Dated 5 May.'

'Good. That would be the copy he bought the day he murdered Nancy Quinn. There is quite enough there, Flora – with what we already have – to prove that he murdered old man Piddington *and* Nancy Quinn.'

'I thought you'd be pleased, sir.'

'Yes, but you haven't found that diamond. We need to find that to be able to wrap this bank robbery well and truly round Reville's neck. Tell me, did SOCO search his body thoroughly?'

'Well, yes, sir. Don Taylor knew you that you particularly wanted to find the diamond.'

'What about the vicar's car?'

'Yes, sir. Don and his team finished that a few minutes ago. It isn't there.'

'Well, keep looking. It has to be found. I can't think where it has got to.'

At four o'clock Angel felt tired, with his eyes closing, and his mind not thinking of what he was trying to write. He knew he wouldn't fall asleep, but he wasn't achieving anything useful either. It had slipped his mind that work had taken up most of the previous night. He phoned Ahmed and told him he was going home. Then he drove himself home, put the car away and let himself in by the back door.

Mary was very pleased to see him. Unusually she was in a night-dress and housecoat. She put her arms round his neck and pulled him towards her to deliver a slow and gentle kiss.

'What are you doing home, darling?' she said.

'I was falling asleep at my desk,' he said. 'Why the housecoat? Been to bed?'

'I thought I would have a nap, but when it came to it, I couldn't get off. We must have an early night tonight.'

'Yeah,' he said, then he went to the fridge and took out a can of German beer. He found a glass on the draining-board and poured it out.

Mary came back up to him and said, 'How's your face?'

'Sore.' Then he said, 'How are your wrists?'

'Sore, but getting better.'

'You are sure he didn't hurt you, sweetheart, aren't you?'

'He scared me. He scared me stiff, but he didn't hurt me. Only my wrists.'

Angel shook his head.

He went through to the sitting room. He sat in his favourite chair for about a minute. He was thinking through the events of the day, and he didn't like what he remembered. Then suddenly, he looked up brightly and said, 'Any post?'

'Two,' Mary said and she went to the sideboard and brought them to him.

He looked at each of them in turn and wrinkled his nose. He reluctantly tore into the first envelope. It consisted of several colourful leaflets.

'Hey up, Mary. I've won a £50 voucher that can be spent at any of the forty-two branches of Warmglow Sunshine Tanning Salon.'

Mary smiled and said, 'Fifty pounds, eh? There's one in town. On Wath Road.'

Angel rubbed his chin. 'Hey. This is addressed to me. It should be addressed to you.'

'No. I've been entering competitions in your name just to prove that you *can* win prizes.'

'Oh? Really? Well, thank you, sweetheart. Let me give you a kiss.'

He kissed her gently on the lips. Then he said, 'But, you know, I'm not into getting myself tanned. You have it.'

Mary wasn't pleased. 'I got it for *you*. It's always the same. You never let me give you *anything* without a lot of argument.'

'When have I the time to go and play about at getting a tan?'

Mary gasped loudly and walked out of the sitting room. She was not pleased.

Angel noticed. As he began to open the second letter he said in a very low voice, 'And I bet you've spent more on postage than the voucher is worth.'

He took the letter out of the second envelope. His face dropped. He looked round. 'Mary,' he called. 'It's from the ruddy gas company.'

Mary put her nose into the room. 'What are you shouting about now?'

'It's from the ruddy gas company. We owe them £192, and gas is going up another 5 per cent at the end of June. What do you think of that?'

'Well, Michael, you've got to be reasonable. It's going up for everybody.'

He put his arms in the air in exasperation and yelled, 'Reasonable? I'm always reasonable. I'm the most reasonable man I know. Here,' he said, handing Mary the suntan voucher and the letter from the gas company. 'Send that to the gas board. Tell them to deduct that from our bill.'

Mary stared at him, not at first realizing what he had said. She sighed.

Angel's mobile rang.

He fumbled down into his pocket, found it and pressed the button. 'Angel.'

'Hello there, Michael.'

Angel recognized the Glaswegian voice of his good friend, Dr Mac. 'You old codger. I hear you've been picking a fight with a madman.'

'Huh. I had to defend myself, Mac, that's all. He picked the fight with me.'

'Aye, so I understand. Well, assuredly he didn't get the better of you. You can still enjoy a dram, whilst he will never again even smell the cork.'

Angel smiled. 'Where is this leading?'

'Oh, just idle chit-chat, an old doctor's subtle way of finding out how you survived that wee punch-up. Your erstwhile opponent has a broken jaw and several nasty contusions to his face. I hope that you gave out more than you got.'

'I really don't know about that, Mac. But rest assured, I'm OK.'

'Good. Good,' Mac said. 'You'll have learned from that, that I have Mr Reville on the slab in front of me.'

'I knew that he was in your accomplished hands,' Angel said with a grin.

'You can cut out the sarcasm, or I shallna tell you what you want to know.'

'All right. I'm listening. Go on.'

'I'm thinking you will be pleased. I took X-rays of his chest, thorax, hip and thigh parts and discovered a perfect hexagonal shadow in his stomach. When I opened him up I found a large clear stone. When I washed it under the tap, it glistened and reflected the most beautiful colours.'

Angel smiled. 'Do you know, Mac? That news is better than any of your bottles of medicine.'